JOSH JOINS THE

ROUNDHEADS

A Josh And Olly Adventure

J.J.Ayton

First published in 2016 by
J. J. Ayton
Barnsley S75 2SS UK

Text © J. J. Ayton 2016
Illustrations © Frank Ayton 2016

The rights of J. J. Ayton to be identified as the author of this work
have been asserted by her in accordance with the Copyright,
Designs and Patents Act 1988.

ISBN 978-0-9576115-2-8

Printed and bound by CPI Group (UK) Ltd, Croydon, CR0 4YY

Dedication

For my grandsons Scott and Kyle, who both like stories.

Acknowledgements

I'd like to thank my first readers, Megan Cattanach, ten years old when she read the first draft of my story, and Olivia Horsfield from Churchfield Primary School. Their comments were invaluable, not least in making me re-write a more exciting beginning. Thanks are due to Rosemary Cattanach, Alison Taft and members of Barnsley Writers who commented regularly on my developing narrative.

Sandra Wynne and Lucy Williams made invaluable comments on my almost final draft.

Lastly, but certainly not least, my thanks go to my husband Frank who produced illustrations outside his usual artistic interests and had to put up with my constant instructions and demands.

1

Josh watched the pikes advancing and heard the menacing beat of the drum. He swayed in time with the marching feet. He felt the heavy weight of the breastplate and sword as he paced shoulder to shoulder with his Roundhead colleagues.

The wooden stand for the audience under his feet gave way to rough grass as the pikes and swords of their enemy drew nearer and he kept pace alongside where he could be most use.

The formation broke. Swords flailed, crashing on leather and steel. The Cavalier line nearly held. His comrades pushed on, seeking to gain ground, knocking opponents out of the way and leaving them sprawled.

Finally Roundheads pushed Cavaliers back, swords flailing leaving more of their opponents lying prone on the ground. Their enemy's barrier, hastily erected, soon gave way and with a hearty roar, the final skirmish began. At last the Roundheads were victorious.

A hand pulled Josh down into his seat and his father's voice spoilt the picture. Now Josh heard cheers and boos as the performers lined up to take their bows. His father's laugh and a nudge from his friend, Olly, broke the spell.

He sighed as he joined in the applause. "I wish I could be a Roundhead. It would be super. The Roundheads were right."

Olly sniggered. "What could you do?"

"I could do something."

Their argument stopped as the leading Roundhead, Captain Harry, addressed the audience. "We Parliamentarians thank you for your support. Please give a cheer for the valiant Royalists. Oliver Cromwell's Parliamentarians were victorious against Sir Roger Bolchester in 1643. He escaped during the battle though his family never lived in Bolchester Castle again. We pray we'll be successful again at our next meet..." He gave details of the date and time and Josh watched the crowd drift away.

2

Josh saw the plank gate standing slightly open. Even though it was held shut by a chain, he could peer through the crack and he gasped at what he saw. Uniforms were lined up on rails waiting by a van - helmets, feathered hats, weapons and armour.

"Out the way, lad." A large man pushed him away and reached for the padlock.

Josh gasped. "What are you doing? Where're you going?"

"You a spy? If I told you I'd be shot."

"Those clothes are for Cavaliers and Roundheads." Josh recognised them. "I know you too." He looked more closely at the man who'd spoken. "I saw you in the Civil War display two weeks ago." The jeans and grubby tee-shirt made the man seem smaller than the soldier he had been.

The man didn't answer.

"You had swords... and pikes. Pikes stopped horses charging. Have you got a gun? Some soldiers had proper guns."

"Go on…"

"Well," Josh frowned at him. "You were the Roundhead leader. I saw you in that battle at that big house. We went to the display. You had the largest sword… and shiny armour. You took their captain prisoner."

The man laughed at him. "You think you know some history then. I'm Harry Smithson and I'm part of the New Model Army. There's Royalists in our society too though we usually call them Cavaliers."

"I'm Josh." He didn't give his surname.

"What else d'you know?"

"There were Roundheads and Cavaliers. The Roundheads' leader was Oliver Cromwell. He ruled after Charles the First. That king was beheaded. But the Roundheads didn't last. Another king came back."

"So, you know your stuff. My soldiers were really called Parliamentarians. See my hair? We Roundheads had short hair and were better fighters. 'Cavaliers' was the Royalists' nickname. There's lots of stories."

"Will you tell them to me? I think the Roundheads were right… not everyone liked them… I want to be a Roundhead."

"You're not old enough. Maybe I'll see you at one of our displays." Harry Smithson laughed as he padlocked the gate behind him. He gave Josh a thumbs up and walked off.

"You should find out more about our general. You've heard of Oliver Cromwell?"

Josh knew a challenge when he heard one.

Josh hung around the society's meeting ground whenever he could. "I'm fourteen... well in October. I know I can't fight but I could do other things."

Ralph Smithson looked at the sturdy, determined figure in front of him. "Only if a society member vouches for you..."

Eventually, Captain Harry Smithson relented. "All right. If you help me with cleaning up after a battle, I'll tell you all about our society... and what really happened in 1642... but you've got to find things out for yourself too."

On many weekends after that first meeting, Josh spent time with Captain Harry, helping to scrape mud off boots and clean armour.

"We Parliamentarians objected to the king raising taxes. He spent them on himself and his favourites at the royal court. We became the New Model Army. Oliver Cromwell was our leader and he picked a general who understood battle tactics. He made all the regiments practise the same skills... and he insisted everyone was paid regularly and looked after."

"What about the Cavaliers?" Josh wanted to know everything.

5

"Well, many of the Royalist army commanders were lazy and some were selfish. They didn't pay their men properly."

"Did they forget?"

"Possibly. Maybe on purpose... Some were just mean."

Josh had already decided. "I'm definitely on the side of the Roundheads."

Captain Harry tried to continue but Josh interrupted. "Why do people think Cavaliers were romantic? I know I'd be badly treated if I'd been a Cavalier... unless I was one of the knights."

"How do you know? What have you learned about our general?"

Josh wanted to be a proper Roundhead. If only Captain Harry would agree.

3

Josh was determined. He waited till his father finished watching the news. "Dad, I need to go on the computer. Please can I?"

"You spend too much time on that thing. Why don't you play football, get outside? At your age..."

"I know, Dad, but mum won't let me go to the park. Please."

"All right, lad... though nothing you can't let me see. Promise?" His father sometimes checked to make sure.

"Yes, Dad."

When Josh tired of researching the Roundheads he had a good game of Minecraft with his mate Olly. If he could find out enough Olly, short for Oliver, could be a Cavalier. He liked the joke with his friend's name. He knew there'd been people from all over the world in England for centuries but wondered if someone with Indian ancestors had ever been in the Civil War.

*****

"You still going on about that Civil War stuff? Come on, there's a good match on the box..."

"But, Dad."

"Enough. You'll ruin your eyes messing about on that computer."

Whenever he could, Josh continued searching. He found a book in his local library and then a leaflet about the Civil War Re-enactment Society. How could he persuade his dad to take him to the next event? He decided to talk to his mum first.

She asked, "What's so interesting about an old battle? We've already seen one."

"It wasn't just any old battle. This one's at Bolchester Castle and it's about fairness and..." He stopped when he saw her grin.

"Talk to your father."

"Dad, can we go? Mum says it's okay." He crossed his fingers.

After some discussion, a family outing was planned.

That night, a strange figure woke Josh for the first time. The man was dressed like a knight with fine clothes and long, curly hair. His clothes showed he was a Cavalier. Who was he and what did he want with him? Josh was still puzzled when he woke the next morning. That knight had seemed so clear.

He forgot his dream and slept soundly for the next

three nights. Then the figure woke him again. This time, when the man appeared, Josh saw he had cruel eyes and an angry stare. He left Josh shaking and breathless. The next time he appeared, the knight was hatless and his clothes were dirty and torn. Josh knew the knight was his enemy and would hurt him if he could. His fixed stare accused him, of something he had done but Josh didn't know what that was. Every time he reappeared, he looked more bedraggled and angry. Josh couldn't escape him.

What did the man want with him? The dreams, and Josh was sure they were dreams, frightened him. He didn't understand why the stranger appeared. Was his visitor trying to tell him something?

When, at last, his next nights were undisturbed, Josh managed to push his worries out of his mind.

4

Olly grumbled when Josh invited him. "It's only history. It's nothing to do with us. Why d'you want to watch blokes in fancy dress pretending to fight?"

"Because the Civil War was a real war. It changed everything."

"But we've already seen them." Olly gave in. Josh was only two months older than him but he used his age advantage for plans like this.

Three Sundays later, Josh and his parents bundled into the car and set off. His friend, Olly, was waiting at his gate. He clambered into the back ignoring his own mum's "Behave yourself, Oliver. And say thank you properly at the end of the day."

Both boys waved as they drove away and Olly immediately started to play a game on his phone while Josh kept time to the beat in his headset. He grinned at Olly but his friend ignored him.

"Right boys. We'll have lunch before we watch the display. Then you can explore. We can meet at the café at half past four."

"Great." Josh grinned.

As usual, they wolfed their food, insisting they needed to get good places at the front. When, at last, all the seats were filled, a drum roll hushed the crowd. A Cavalier, in velvet coat and broad brimmed hat bowed low to the audience.

A voice on the loudspeaker announced. "Ladies and gentlemen - Sir Roger Bolchester, owner of this castle."

The knight spoke. "Ladies and gentlemen... honourable friends... we supporters of Charles the First, the king..."

Josh's mouth went dry as he recognised the clothes of his nightmare enemy.

"There's Sir Roger. We'll have him this time!" A troop of Roundheads surrounded the knight.

Olly gasped. "Let him go. That's not fair."

There was a laugh from the people around them and, this time, Josh pulled Olly back onto his seat. Then it was the turn of the Roundheads to be attacked. Cavaliers, armoured and some mounted on horses, entered the parade ground and the sound of hooves grew. The society's soldiers had practised their manoeuvres but now rehearsals were behind them. Olly supported the Cavaliers and urged them on but once again the Roundheads were the victors and then the boys were free to explore.

The rest of the castle beckoned. They chose a staircase

which spiralled up into the first tower.

At the top, "Look at that!" Olly pointed towards the distant landscape. The mewl of a buzzard echoed as it circled above the fields and hedgerows. He watched the bird, its wings hardly moving as it floated on a thermal breeze.

"It's hunting," Olly whispered, fascinated by the bird's performance. "We did winds in science. That bare field heats up quickly and then hot air rises. Birds use it"

"So do gliders. My dad explained it to me." For the moment, Josh forgot about Sir Roger's bad deeds. He wasn't going to be outdone. "They didn't know about that when people came here. They used birds for hunting. Come on."

The bird no longer held Josh's interest but Olly leaned against the stonework still enjoying the views. Josh left him and followed the turret wall out onto the battlements. He knew Olly would trail after him.

Outside the castle walls the ground fell away steeply. They looked all around. "Look out there. Nobody could creep up if you had a sentry up here." Olly traced the ridges and valleys of the crenellated wall with his hand. "This is good. You could hide behind these high bits and shoot at the enemy through the gaps."

"Everyone knows that," Josh wasn't impressed.

Josh leaned out peering at the side of the next tower

and pointed.

"Look, Olly, There's slits in the walls for archers…"

"Come on. There's an attendant watching. We'll get sent down if you stay there." Olly grabbed Josh's sweater to pull him back.

Josh grunted, "Let me go. I'm fine. Look at those people moving behind the openings." But he was careful to walk properly staying close to the stonework as they followed the outer wall to the next tower.

He smiled at the steward who scowled back. "Stay safe or you're out."

The boys grinned at each other when their watcher looked the other way.

"This is as wide as a lane. That must be why there's only a low wall on the inner side.

"There's no danger up here… it's your own side down there. The danger comes from outside." Josh pointed away from the inner courtyard and back over the battlements. "It's still steep outside. This is a really good place… I wish I'd lived here when it was a proper castle."

"Then you'd have been a Cavalier and the Roundheads would have killed you in battle. You heard them at the display."

Josh couldn't think of an answer for that especially as he knew Sir Roger hated him. By then, they'd reached the second tower. "Shall we carry on round the top or go down through it?" He gave his friend the choice.

"Down."

So they tramped down steps taking care to keep to the outer wall where the treads were wider, through three levels, to the ground floor. They were disappointed that each level held nothing but bare rooms with oak plank floors and stone walls. They saw nothing to suggest the wealth and glory of the past.

"There's nothing there. It's boring."

"There's not much in the courtyard either. There's only those stone outlines where the kitchens and outbuildings used to be. What's in the next tower?"

"The next one's got proper rooms with things in." Josh set off across the grass. He knew Olly would follow. They'd been friends for ages and Josh usually had the best ideas.

"How do you know?"

Josh couldn't answer but sensed Sir Roger calling to him from his private rooms. He needed to go there but what for?

"You'll see," he said and ducked through the courtyard entrance.

"D'you think they had a one-way system - up one tower and down the next?" Olly didn't expect an answer, just hurried to keep up, as usual.

14

5

Josh led the climb up the next staircase. They stopped at each landing and every doorway and peered in briefly. On the top level, they found a grand chamber. It had the same layout as they'd already seen on the lower floors.

All the walls were still wood panelled and, in some places, they saw the remains of painted patterns. In this room, a great stone fireplace nearly filled the middle wall.

"That's clever." Josh pointed to the clawed feet of a bird carved into the fireplace.

"That's the Bolchester coat of arms. Don't touch it... it's hard to clean marble."

Once again they'd not noticed a steward.

"What's it all mean?" Olly ignored the tug at his back. Josh had spotted a second doorway and wandered off.

Olly listened as the attendant explained. "It's a shield because the lord of the castle was a knight. Only knights carried shields. The bird's an eagle representing a man of action. There you can see a castle and a lion. They stand for strength of spirit, you know, courage."

Olly was hooked.

Josh strolled into a smaller, panelled room. The windows from both rooms faced away from any direct sunlight so the space was dim. He worked out that a small fireplace backed onto the large one in the main room.

Josh turned slowly, examining the faded patterns on the panelling. A large portrait decorated one wall. He gasped when he saw the full length painted figure, its boots at Josh's eye level. Josh read the label, Sir Roger Bolchester, the name of the Royalist leader he'd just seen captured in the re-enactment. As he looked closer he recognised the knight from his nightmare. Both his dream figure and this portrait were dressed in the same fancy clothes; identical crimson knee length trousers and a blue jacket with lace cuffs and collar. This man had the same trim beard and dark hair spilling onto his shoulders. He wore a wide brimmed hat, its two long black feathers curling onto his collar. This face was severe and unsmiling. This knight was important and Josh knew the man threatened him. He gasped when he saw the knight's dark eyes. They read his thoughts.

The nightmare Cavalier had called him 'traitor'. This portrait did the same. This knight hated him. Josh shuddered. He didn't know what to do.

"You're the traitor. I believe in Parliament. Fairness for

everybody," he shouted.

The portrait eyes held his gaze and bored into him. He shivered as he recognised hatred and fear on the face and backed away, moving faster than he realised. His heel caught on the uneven slab floor and he toppled backwards against a wall.

The panelling gave way and he pitched into a narrow stone chamber. He saw nothing. The panelling had closed behind him.

6

After his fall, Josh's problems continued. He cracked his head as he tried to stand. His forehead hurt and his head throbbed. He winced as movement made him dizzy.

He was walled into a narrow passage, rough wood along one side and stone on the other. He reached up to the ceiling. More stone. He just had room to turn so felt behind. He could only move one way. Unless he could find a way out, he was trapped. Tears filled his eyes and he swallowed hard. Crying wouldn't help him. He had to be brave. He had to plan.

Something about the rough wood seemed familiar. He fingered it and found joins. Though the wood was splintery it was solid. Was he the wrong side of the panelled wall? Josh rubbed at his head again and something tickled his face - linen. A blue sweatshirt sparked his memory. He felt his clothes. He wore woollen breeches and a sleeveless jerkin over a collared shirt. This felt wrong but he didn't know why. He'd think about it later. For now he needed to escape this trap he was in.

He recalled a panelled room. His head ached as he tried to work out what had happened. That was it. A wooden panel had given way and he'd fallen through it before it had closed behind him. Why was everything so muddled?

He could feel rough wood so worked out that the carpenters had only polished the panels facing the room. He was behind them with a stone wall at his back. He felt all round but there was no sign of any opening. He was trapped. Tears filled his eyes and he swallowed hard. Crying wouldn't help him. He had to be brave. He had to plan.

That was when he felt a draught. It was only a slight movement of air but it was a clue. It might lead him to a way out. He dropped onto all fours and crawled along the wall alongside the panelling. He was in a narrow tunnel and could only go one way.

The ground sloped as Josh crawled on. He inched his way forwards being careful to feel for the sides, floor and roof before he moved far. He must be in a secret passage.

Josh bumped his head again and his hands slipped as the floor sloped more steeply downwards. There the wood gave way to stone on both sides.

He should have paid more attention as he crawled.

He'd no idea how far he'd come, just knew that he still couldn't stand. He knew Bolchester Castle was a Royalist stronghold but couldn't remember why he'd been in the castle. Maybe he'd been sent to count the enemy. Perhaps he'd nearly been discovered and that had forced him to hide.

He moved cautiously. Here the draught was stronger. The cold air ruffled his hair. It must be coming from outside. He moved carefully, feeling his way as the passage sloped lower all the time. The air grew colder still and he continued until his hand pressed against the end of the tunnel.

Here the roof dropped to about sixty centimetres above floor level, high enough to crawl through but too low to stand. He felt a large, stone block marking the end of the tunnel but the draught came from around its base near the floor. He pressed hard against it but nothing happened and he slipped and nearly banged his head. Carefully he felt all around the block until he found a narrow slot at one edge. His fingers just fitted in and he touched some sort of catch. If wind could get in maybe he could get out. This secret tunnel must have a secret exit.

Something clicked and the stone moved slightly. He pushed again but nothing happened but when he slid one finger further in he found a lever and pulled backwards. The block began to move. He pushed at the latch side and the stone swung sideways. There was an opening.

He stretched out on his tummy and slid forwards until his shoulders were over the edge. He wriggled further, feeling for ground and touched earth less than an arm's length below him. It stretched as far as he could reach so it seemed safe. He wriggled forward until he could scramble out on to grass. He'd no way of knowing where he was. He just hoped it wasn't where a Cavalier might see and capture him.

He knelt at first then stood slowly, one hand above his head checking the space. He could stand. He straightened his legs, eased his back and took a deep breath of fresh air. That crawl had been harder than he thought.

He looked around, blinking although the light was dim. He was at the base of the tower and at the top of a long slope. Daylight was fading and the castle tower blotted out the setting sun leaving a deep shadow on the grass.

Josh scrambled to his feet. As he started to run, he heard the stone grind shut behind him. He was on his own unless he could find his own troop of Roundheads. A brief memory of a gate with a padlock slithered by and was gone. Somehow he knew he had to find Captain Harry, his commander.

7

OLLY

In the large castle chamber, Olly turned to say, "Did you know that those designs meant all that? I wonder if there are...?" He was talking to himself. "Josh! Josh, where are you? Did you see him go?"

The steward shrugged. "There's more to see in the other chambers. He may have gone down."

Olly looked around carefully, checked the second smaller room and glanced at the full-size portrait. The Cavalier stared back. Olly didn't notice how his lip curled in a smirk.

He carried on down the stairs, less careful than before until his foot slipped on a smoothed and narrow step. He grabbed the rail to prevent a tumble. There were still lots of steps to go and only small landings. He could have broken something. From then on he held onto the handrail until he reached the next level. Again an elegantly furnished room opened before him. But Josh wasn't there, nor in the smaller side room.

"That one's a retiring room. The lady of the manor used that when she wanted to relax. She'd embroider or work on her tapestry. It's called a solar."

Olly shuffled impatiently, too polite to rush off while the steward, this time a lady, was in full flow.

"Did you see another boy here? Like me but with ginger hair..."

"No. I've only seen families today..." but Olly had left before she finished.

The chamber at the bottom of the tower held more of the furniture which had once been used by Lord Bolchester and his family. This room still had wrinkled, coloured glass in the windows. The small leaded panes rationing the light in reds and yellows.

"...and original only in this room. We've had to re-glaze all the windows in the upper rooms..." A guide was leading a tour but Josh wasn't there either.

Olly looked all round the central courtyard. Now it was full of other visitors, couples and families but no boys on their own. He scanned the upper walkways between the towers but the afternoon was drawing in and a chill breeze kept the few visitors he saw scurrying from one tower to the next, but no Josh.

Josh had played silly tricks on him before - jumping out from behind cupboards and doors at school; hiding under his computer station and pinching his knees so that he yelled and got told off for silliness, but nothing like this. He'd never just abandoned him. If Josh was hiding somewhere, waiting for him to be really anxious before he jumped out laughing at him, he'd never speak to him again.

Olly decided to search all the towers. Josh must be somewhere. "He'll not play a stupid trick like that again... trying to worry me... though I'm not really worried..."

"Sorry, were you talking to me?" A woman carrying a toddler on her hip made him jump.

"Oh... no... sorry. I'm looking for my friend. He's hiding. He's the same height as me but he's got ginger hair..."

"Sorry, dear. You're the only boy on his own... I've not seen anyone else..."

Olly didn't wait to hear any more. He ran up the stairs in the next tower, stopping at each landing to make a quick circuit of every room before climbing onwards.

At the top of every staircase he checked the lookout points then followed the battlements to the next tower, this time reversing his search by hurrying down through the levels, making sure always to walk on the widest side of the step.

By the time he got round to the furnished tower again he wavered between anger and anxiety. Josh could think up stupid stunts but he usually gave up long before this.

Once again, the steward in the fireplace room replied, "No, no ginger headed boy has been here... in fact, you were the last young lad I've seen in here today. Isn't it time you went home?"

Olly trudged back down to the courtyard. A clock chimed the hour and he knew it would soon be time to meet with Josh's parents. If Josh was there laughing at him, he'd thump him... but he couldn't, not with Josh's parents looking on.

He wouldn't cry. 'Stupid boy'... that's what that fellow on the telly said... the one in the programme his mum always laughed at. Who was stupid, Josh or him?

8

Olly searched the battlements and tower rooms three times. At first he'd retraced the route he and Josh had taken together. Then he reversed it. After that he'd visited the kitchen building, the stables and other buildings within the walls. He even walked through the restaurant and the gift shop, checking both sides of every display. One of the counter assistants watched him carefully and began to follow him every time he disappeared behind a set of shelves.

"I've lost my friend... I thought he was in here."

The assistant nodded but still watched him until he left the shop. After that, he went back to the first tower they'd climbed and started again. No one realised how worried he was.

By now there were fewer visitors to be seen and some of the stewards had left their posts and were laughing and chatting in the top room of the second tower.

"Haven't you found your friend yet?" One of the women asked.

Another 'tutted' in sympathy and said "This would be a

grand place to play hide and seek."

"Have you both got 'phones?" a third, a man, asked.

"I've tried... and tried but I just get 'number unavailable' every time. We've got to meet his mum and dad by the café really soon."

They all checked the time on their phones or watches. The first lady tried to reassure him. "He's sure to turn up by then. The café shuts at five and the castle closes at six. He'll have to leave with you then." She was very sure.

Olly nodded at her and hurried out to search all the towers again.

He searched the courtyard buildings again, this time double checking every doorway, inspecting both sides of each opening, ducking to examine the inside of every oven. No Josh. His thoughts whirled. He'd never speak to Josh again. Josh must be lying injured. Maybe he'd fallen off the walls.

When he saw Josh's parents sitting on a bench and looking as if they were enjoying the sight of the pennants fluttering brightly from a corner tower, he made for the walls careful not to attract their attention. This time his progress was very slow. He took his time looking up and down each stairwell, listening for the sound of any footsteps which could hint that Josh was still teasing him.

Olly entered every chamber and now they were empty.

He walked along each wall feeling for loose blocks or hidden crannies. He even clambered inside the great stone fireplaces to see if Josh had climbed inside and twice he cracked his head on the boarding blocking off the chimney.

At the furnished tower, the attendant in the middle chamber scowled. "Isn't it time you went home? You've been in here three times. What's the attraction?"

"I'm still looking for my friend."

"Well, he's not here and I've not seen any other lad on his own except you. Now - buzz off! It's nearly closing time. I want my tea, not to wait around for you."

He was luckier on the top floor. That steward had gone so he searched every corner, even peering inside the chimney again. Then he had a better idea. He started by the door once more and this time walked around the smaller room again tapping at the panelling. At the first corner he heard footsteps and stood quietly until he heard voices from the next room and two stewards clattered down the stairs.

When he looked again he saw Josh's parents still sitting on the bench but checking their watches and looking all round. He ducked away from that window careful not to attract their attention.

He restarted his experiment and went back to the room where he'd last seen Josh. Close to the outer wall he thought the sound changed. He retraced a few steps and tapped his way forward again. The sound definitely changed but though he felt all round the panelling, there was no way it would open. The panelling on the third, window wall was solid but this time he saw the huge painting of the knight between the windows. The portrait on the wall peered down at him but offered no help. It seemed unfriendly. Olly shook his head. Now he was imagining things. He was even more worried when he peered through the window and saw Josh's parents strolling across the courtyard towards their meeting place.

Olly followed the stairs until he reached the bottom of the last tower and his progress slowed. He took his time listening at each stairwell for the sound of any footsteps which could suggest that Josh was still teasing him then, at the bottom of the last tower, he ducked into the kitchens for one last look.

When he next saw Josh's parents they were standing by the path to the café. Mr Banks was looking at his watch and his wife was scanning the walkway.

Olly took a deep breath and went to meet them. What could he say? If he told them Josh was hiding from him they would worry and if he said Josh was hiding from them they'd be cross. He'd been worried for the last hour. Josh was his best friend but right now he hated him. He really wanted to thump him. Josh wasn't playing fair.

"Ah! There you are... and only five minutes late. Where's Josh?"

He couldn't help it. A tear escaped and ran down his cheek. "I don't know. I've been looking for him for ages. I'm sure something's wrong."

"No." Mr Banks patted his shoulder. "He always plays stupid tricks. He'll jump out on us if we start to look worried. Come on." Then added very loudly so Josh would hear. "We'll have a cup of tea before the café closes... he'll not want to miss out on a drink and a bun."

Olly followed them thankful Josh was no longer just his problem though he knew Josh would sulk if he was in trouble. Olly still felt something was wrong.

Mrs Banks eyed him thoughtfully. She recognised how worried he was. She checked her watch, ten to five. "I'll give Josh ten minutes to appear. If he's not reappeared I'll get him paged on the public address system. All right?" She waited for Olly's nod then continued, "Now... there's time for that chocolate brownie... you like those..."

Olly nodded and thanked her for his refreshments but the brownie, moist and sticky and just how he usually liked them, stuck in his throat and tasted of sawdust.

9

Mrs Banks glanced at her husband, nodded towards Olly and sent him the silent question 'Have they had a big bust up?'

Josh's dad shrugged in reply but as the time passed they both fidgeted in their seats, turning to peer through the windows and doorway, willing Josh to appear. At twenty past five they rose from their seats. Olly left the remains of the brownie. It had stuck in his throat though he'd gulped down a drink of apple juice. Without a word, the three of them left the café. Mrs Banks spotted one of the attendants and pointed him out. Mr Banks approached him.

"I'm afraid we've mislaid our son. He's been hiding from his friend most of the afternoon. How can we put out a call for him... we need to go home."

The attendant indicated Olly. "I saw him looking for his friend earlier. I was on duty in that tower." He pointed it out. "You better come with me."

The steward led them to an office and explained the situation to the woman sitting at a computer.

"I'm the manager here. Just sit down and I'll make a start. Give me all the details... his name, age... what he was wearing?"

Mr and Mrs Banks looked at each other in alarm while the manager picked up a phone and made a call, lowering her voice so they couldn't hear what she said. Then she told the steward to remain with the small group. That wasn't reassuring.

A second phone call was clearer. "Jane Garrett here. Please put out a call for Josh Banks to go to the nearest attendant. Whoever finds him, radio as soon as he makes contact and bring him to my office. It's time for Josh to go home."

A clock on the wall ticked and the sound grew louder as they waited. The phone rang. Jane Garrett answered, "I'll deal with the figures later. Please leave this line clear until we've found this missing boy."

Mrs Banks sniffed and pretended she had a tickle in her nose. Mr Banks put his arm round her. Olly didn't have anyone to hug him.

More castle staff arrived and were given areas to search. "We do know all the little corners where someone small could hide," one muttered.

That comment made Olly so cross that for a moment he forgot to worry. "Josh's not small... he's as tall as me."

Ms Garrett and another steward looked at him then at each other and Olly could see they wanted to smile. He scowled at them.

"You don't believe me. You think it's just a silly trick. I've been looking for Josh all afternoon. We were in that tower room with furniture and the fancy fireplace."

This time he couldn't stop the tears and Mrs Banks slid an arm around his shoulder.

"I was there, Jane." Another castle person appeared. "I was on duty when the boys arrived. I remember this lad coming back to me and asking if I'd seen his friend. That was about an hour after the display ended."

Mrs Banks hugged Olly and stared at her husband who looked as if he might be sick. That was a long time for a boy to play a stupid joke on everyone. Something must be wrong.

Jane Garrett took charge again. "John," this was the attendant who'd just arrived, "You go back to where you know you saw both boys. Take one of the others with you and double check everywhere. That tower is the only furnished one so look in all the cupboards and chests. It's possible he could have climbed in to hide and wasn't strong enough to lift the lid."

"There's a hollow panel..." but Olly got no further. He was ignored as the remaining attendants were allocated places to search and the castle manager ensured that they met up with each other in such a way, no nook could have been missed.

"I'll stay here with Mr and Mrs Banks," she ignored Olly's presence. "Report back here when you're sure you've covered every spot. Make sure your radios are turned on. You'll be recalled as soon as someone finds him."

As an afterthought she added, "...and I've alerted the car park staff. They're checking every car with children in."

Olly was even more unhappy then because, with everyone looking for Josh, he was ignored. Mr and Mrs Banks seemed to have forgotten all about him.

When the castle and its grounds closed, the car park staff reported that all the visitors had left. Most of the staff had joined in the search and Olly was left alone.

One of the café ladies remembered him. "Here, duck. This will take your mind off everything for five minutes," and gave him a slice of flapjack. "There'll be more made fresh in the morning so this one needn't be wasted." She patted his shoulder and left him to it.

Olly took a bite but it was difficult to swallow. He couldn't enjoy it without Josh. He was the only one who'd known that Josh was properly lost when he hadn't arrived at their meeting place.

He tried again to tell the manager about the hollow

sounding panel but she only said, "We're doing everything we can. Try not to worry."

'How do you stop?' he wondered.

Everyone was busy phoning in or coming to the office to report progress but nobody spoke to him. Then Miss Garrett went out to speak to one of the searchers. That's when he saw Mr and Mrs Banks talking to a police officer. Olly had already repeated over and over all he knew. He decided he'd have to do something. He couldn't wait in the manager's office any longer.

He found a piece of paper and wrote ' I'm going to the last tower where I saw him.' He remembered to sign it 'Olly' and put it on the manager's desk. No one noticed him go.

10

As he crossed the courtyard, he did wonder how so many people, so busy looking for a boy his height, could ignore his progress. Had anyone even noticed him?

His legs ached from climbing stairs so many times as he staggered into the large furnished chamber. The lights were still on but the steward had gone. He paused to look at the carved fireplace. If he hadn't been so absorbed in the heraldic symbols he would have seen Josh go. He'd have spotted him if he'd tried to climb into the fireplace. Anyway, it was boarded, blocking the opening completely. Olly scrambled inside and peered up then he tapped every wooden panel, just to be sure.

When he finished he went into the anteroom, the one Olly thought of as the portrait room. He stepped into the centre and slowly scanned the walls. He remembered the portrait face. Now it seemed to be frowning. He was sure it had been smiling last time he'd looked. He shook his head to clear it.

He didn't go straight to the wall where he'd found the hollow sound. Just to be sure, he tapped his way round and knocked on each panel in turn moving slowly all round the room, listening carefully but every wooden panel was solid. When he heard a different, hollow sound he started from the doorway again and left that wall to last.

This time he started in one corner and rapped every few centimetres moving towards the centre. He had tested more than half the panels before the sound changed. He stepped back and tapped where he'd been. Solid. He moved forward and there was that hollow sound again. He carried on and searched the full length of the wall. The hollow section was very small.

How big, how tall was it? He started again at floor level and knocked again until he reached his hip height. He heard the hollow sound again. The height of one large square section of panelling sounded hollow, different from all the rest. The square was just big enough for a grown up to get through. Maybe there was a hiding space behind if there was a way of opening it. Had Josh worked out how to do so? Had he climbed through?

Olly poked and prodded at the panel. Nothing moved. He stepped to the side so that the light shone directly on the wood and looked closely at each edge of the square. When he examined the panels he could see a difference at both edges but it was so tiny, no one would notice. He'd searched so carefully but only just seen the joins.

There must be an opening. He just had to work out how to find it. He couldn't even get a finger nail into the cracks so there must be a secret fastener.

Olly pressed at the edge of the wood, first on the left, then on the right. Next he tried the top and the bottom. If it was a doorway it didn't yield. He pushed against the panel. Nothing moved. He pressed hard along each side. It was solid. Olly was convinced this was where Josh had disappeared. Frustrated with his lack of success he gave a great kick to the centre of the square. He didn't care if he damaged the wood.

He nearly left then, intending to return to the office, but a slight creak alerted him. He turned back to the wall. There was a tiny gap at one side, narrower than his little finger, and so small he nearly missed it. But the panel had moved. He pushed it with the flat of his hand and it moved a little further. He reached around it and found a latch of some sort on the inside. He pushed the panel further and though it opened, it immediately swung back and clicked shut.

Olly was back where he started but this time he knew he'd been right. But how had he and Josh made the door open and, if it wouldn't stay open, how safe was it to go through?

It must have been his kick. It had been a great thump to the centre of the square. He'd also felt a latch so if he climbed through, he thought he could get back. He experimented.

He kicked the door again and the opening reappeared. This time he felt the back of the wood more carefully. He could feel some sort of spring loaded bolt. There was a catch on the solid part of the wall it would slide into. He practised unlocking the catch and felt it spring back to lock the door again every time he let it go. He decided he'd be safe enough now he knew how to get out. He could explore further.

He climbed through the gap and had a moment of panic when the panel shut behind him. He discovered a tunnel and crawled some way along it. He moved slowly, taking care to avoid the rough edges on the floor slabs. He hadn't gone far when he panicked again. What if the panel stuck? He backed the way he'd come until he reached the door. There was no passage going the other way, just the one route.

He tested the door catch and, for a moment it didn't move then opened as before. He let out the breath he'd been holding. Now he knew he'd not get trapped inside.

He crawled on again, this time seeing a tiny glint of light ahead. If there was daylight the tunnel must lead somewhere. He stumbled as his clothing caught against rough stones and splintery wood. He shook himself free and worried some more. His sweatshirt sleeve now felt like velvet. His jeans ended below his knees and were made of rough wool like the knickerbockers he'd seen in paintings. What had happened to him?

If Josh had explored behind the panel how far had he gone? He crawled further and saw a narrow streak of light. Josh must have gone this way. All he had to do was find him.

Olly kept crawling. Even with the distant gleam of light it felt as if the tunnel would never end. He was sure Josh must be in the passage but where? The floor dipped under his hands and he could feel a draught. He took more care. He was definitely moving downhill but where was he going? He jerked to a stop as one hand landed on a stone and he banged his head, "Ow, ow! Ouch."

The noise startled him but it was his own voice distorted by the echo. He rubbed at his head and blew on his hand. He'd found an opening. He knew he had to climb out but didn't know why.

He saw he was on a steep hillside, a cave entrance behind him. Below, he could see a camp and, at its edge, he saw a boy.

11

JOSH

Josh had to find Captain Harry but where to start? He checked there was no one else about then hurried down the slope. He had to stay safe. The scent of the camp fires gave Josh his first clue. If he kept the wind on his face he'd find someone. With luck he'd easily find his own company.

He dropped to the ground while he decided where to go. He needed to report that Sir Roger Bolchester was strengthening his castle. Captain Harry Smithson trusted him. He needed this information.

Josh saw faint traces of smoke above trees and stopped, struck by a thought. This might be his Parliamentarian group but it could be Royalists. Royalists were usually left to forage for themselves. He'd have to be very careful.

He crossed the last of the open ground at a run then paused at the edge of the wood. He smelt wood smoke, acrid from wet branches but overlaid with the aroma of roasting meat.

'Please let it be my troop,' he muttered. The scent reminded him how hungry he was.

He moved quietly using trees and shrubs as cover and treading carefully to avoid cracking branches or rustling leaves. All the time he watched for lookouts. He reached a small clearing. The trees thinned out as he approached and he could see movement but no sentries.

A red squirrel scampered across the clearing, stopped, cocked its head, looked straight at him and scrambled up the nearest tree. Josh nearly laughed out loud at that but stopped himself in time.

He tiptoed across the space and chose a mature oak to hide behind. The group round the campfire was not large, about thirty, Josh thought, but he couldn't count accurately because they moved about. 'So, it's a Royalist camp. Captain Harry needs to know about this too.'

The smell of food had attracted insects. Josh now saw two Cavaliers flapping at them with their plumed hats.

'I hope they get bitten - maybe it will spoil their aim if they have to scratch.' He grinned at the picture he imagined. Then he realised he would be fired at if he was spotted.

He heard, "Fill your plates and gather round."

The gaggle of men surrounded their cook then sat on the ground at the feet of a man who was clearly their officer. His clothes seemed no different from the rest except, Josh saw, that his coat was a rich blue. His hair was long and curling onto his shoulders. It was Sir Roger Bolchester, the man in that castle portrait, the man from his nightmares and the Roundhead's enemy. Sir Roger was organising his next attack.

As Josh tried to work out why the painted portrait had threatened him, he forgot to listen closely. He concentrated again when he heard the speaker say "...and we'll go west before sunrise. Though there are more of them, we can surprise them before they wake up. Right, men. Eat up and dowse the fire. You'll sleep in the wood and set out with the dawn chorus. It's not far over that hill. I'll be back before daybreak so make sure you're ready. Here's to success tomorrow." The officer raised a silver goblet and drank to his men. They grasped leather tankards, raised them and drank.

Josh had heard enough. He had to get out of the wood and fast, and now he knew which way to go.

The faintest tinge of gold showed over the crest of the next hill so that way was west. He picked his way from tree to tree. Whenever he checked, he could still see the men eating but one stood, stretched and bent to speak to one of his companions before creeping into the wood.

Josh dropped to the ground and held his breath but the man went into the bushes away from him. There was a shout and a bellow of laughter which was rapidly silenced. Josh took a chance. He scuttled on all fours, keeping low and using any cover he could find until he reached open ground on the western edge of the woodland.

Though he knew which way to go, he couldn't set off immediately. He'd be seen crossing open ground so he had to wait till it was completely dark. Could he reach his friends in time?

12

Josh waited at the edge of the wood until the sun had completely disappeared. Then he scrambled rapidly across the open ground.

He fell twice. The first time he stumbled over a tiny shrub; the second, he caught his foot in a rabbit hole. He'd have to be careful or he'd spend the night in the open with a broken leg and be captured as a spy when the Cavaliers set out.

He slowed at a hill, straining to see if there was an easy path to the top but also because the sound of his panting would carry on the night air.

By the time he reached the summit, it was dark with just a faint sprinkling of starlight. He was lucky for a moon would have silhouetted him as he crossed the ridge.

He stopped just below the summit trying to gauge the direction he should take and thought he detected a vague movement in the next valley. That must be the camp. Once again, he picked his way with care and breathed thankfully when he reached level ground. He could still see slight movements and knew he was getting close. His luck was in. He'd made it.

A hand landed heavily on his shoulder jerking him to a stop. It forced him back. Then a punch knocked him off his feet and sent him toppling backwards onto the grass. A leather boot on his chest pinned him down. He couldn't breathe properly with that weight on him.

Josh barely saw anything of the figure towering above him. He couldn't make out the uniform or headgear or weapons. If he'd fallen into the hands of a Cavalier scout he was done for.

His captor checked him for weapons, his foot still pressing him down. When the sentry was satisfied he stepped back.

"On your feet, lad. Don't run or I'll skewer you," and he prodded Josh with the end of his weapon.

"Right, lad. Explain yourself. It better be good. You know what happens to spies."

Josh shivered, trying to sort out his words, his head full of memories of mock fights, portraits and traitors' heads on city walls. So many ideas crammed into his head.

But when Josh tried to explain, his captor shook his head. "You. Don't tell lies. The less you say, the least trouble you're in. Just hold your tongue until you've been dealt with."

How could Josh convince them? If no one listened to him the camp would be overrun by sunrise.

"Please take me to Captain Harry."

"What do you know of Captain Harry? Think you can talk your way out of trouble? You've just proved you've been spying on us. Good job I caught you before you could give us away."

"But - "

"Enough!" And this time the guard tied a large kerchief round his mouth gagging him. It was all Josh could do to breathe never mind talk.

A second soldier approached and looked hard at him.

"Caught him spying on us," explained Josh's guard.

"Hmm... I'm sure I've seen him before. What does he say for himself?"

Josh knew the man. The castle parade ground came and went in his mind. He was one of Captain Harry's lieutenants called Matthew. He tried to mumble through his gag but the first soldier gave him a thump.

"Silence. We'll deal with you in good time." He turned to his companion and continued, "I'll tie him in one of the carts. We'll decide where to take him when the cap'n gets here."

Matthew stared at him. "I still think I know him... Right, Henry. Let's get him to the carts. Not long now to daybreak."

'And capture,' thought Josh and he gulped. His mouth was dry and he felt tears of frustration run down his cheek. He shook them away. He didn't want the soldiers to think they frightened him. If only he could get to the captain. He was helpless as the soldier called Henry gave him a shove. Captain Harry would vouch for him... if he wasn't killed in the attack that was coming.

They reached the place where the wagons and horses were bunched together at the edge of the camp. It was not a place that could be defended easily.

"Come on, Henry, we're needed. Time for orders."

"A moment."

Henry, the one who had captured him, grabbed his hands and tied them together behind his back. Josh tried to kick him away but instead, coughed in pain when a punch to his chest left him winded. He staggered and fell. The soldier tied his ankles, lifted him as easily as he would a bag of apples and heaved him into the back of one of the carts.

The wood was old and splintery and caught at his clothes as he was tumbled in. At first Josh lay winded and hurting. He'd bumped his head again when the soldier dropped him over the side and it took him a moment before he could think clearly. If he could get free he'd have to decide what to do but he had to escape first. He wriggled onto his side and bent his legs back until his fingers felt the cord around his ankles. He began to pull at it until he could feel the knot but then he had to straighten out and stretch.

It took several attempts before he managed to unpick the first knot. His back hurt and he had to stretch out again but that small success spurred him on. He didn't know how long it took but by the time his feet were untied, the sky was beginning to lighten. He had to hurry. He had to find someone who would believe him.

Then he had an idea. He'd seen people in strange costumes entertaining the crowds in the market square. Again he struggled with a memory of the square full of cars, and people in different clothes - jeans and sweatshirts. He tried to work out what that meant but then remembered the acrobats. One had jumped backwards and forwards through his linked hands. If Josh could get his arms under his bottom he should be able to wriggle his legs through. It was a struggle but finally he managed it though his wrists were sore from straining to bring them to the front of his body. He lay in the bottom of the wagon getting his breath back and letting the pain in his wrists and shoulders calm down before he started on his next task. At least he could pull away the rag round his mouth. At last he could breathe properly. He used his teeth to work at the cord around his wrists concentrating hard until the sound of approaching footsteps alerted him.

Two blackened faces peered over the side of the cart. "Told you I heard something," said the first.

"Looks like one of ours. How did he get himself captured so quickly?"

"Maybe he got taken prisoner when those Roundheads marched through Windlesthorpe. They said there were Cavalier supporters there.

"Right. Let's leave him here for now. The rest of the troop's almost here. We'll certainly surprise them this time. Come on, there's no time to untie his hands..."

Now he was back where he started but, if he was freed by a troop of Cavaliers, it would be even harder to reach Captain Harry.

13

Then Josh heard rustling noises coming nearer, very quiet but still audible. He struggled with his bonds as he strained to hear who was approaching. The sound was little more than a fresh breeze whipping leaves and grass, so faint no one in the camp could possibly notice. The soldier called Henry knew he was here but would he believe him when fighting started. The battle wasn't lost yet. He needed to warn his own side. Though his hands were still tied he had his voice back.

He decided to call. "Help! Look out! There's some one coming."

He daren't shout that it was the king's men, Royalists, approaching for that lot would kill him if they arrived first. On the other hand, his own side might think he was warning the Royalists. Now he'd made himself a target for both sides. He cowered again in the bottom of the cart and gnawed more urgently at his restraints.

A head peered over the planking beside him, one from his own side, the one called Henry. "I knew I should have skewered you. Shut your mouth. We'll have no more of that noise. I'd kill you now but..."

The rest of his sentence disappeared and Josh saw Henry's hand slide from the wooden planking. He heard a thud and a hurried "Shh... quietly... don't alert the camp."

A different face loomed over him and Josh recognised it as belonging to a sentry from the Royalist camp, one he'd been careful to avoid. This time he was trapped. He stared at the soldier and decided silence would serve him best. Instead he held up his arms so the soldier could see the cord still cutting into his wrists.

"Well lad, we'll soon have you out of there. You did us a good turn... we hadn't spotted that sentry."

Josh gulped. He was now responsible for the death or capture of one of his own and probably the capture of the whole unit. What was worse, the Royalists thought he supported them and he'd never get to Captain Harry. If he did, the Parliamentarians would brand him a traitor.

"I'm Gilbert. Our commander will want to see you himself... he'll be very pleased. Could have lost several men if you hadn't warned us."

"Who's your commander... I mean... what's his name, I've never met him before."

"You'll recognise him when you see him. He's a grand man... Sir Roger Bolchester."

Josh's gasp interrupted the explanation. "Oh... Sorry... it's the cord... my hands... didn't mean... I've heard about Sir Roger but I've only seen him in the distance."

"Oh, yes. Everyone round these parts knows him. He's one of the king's best officers. He's a good man if you're on his side. It's not so good for those Roundheads... Cromwell's army. Why can't they dress properly like gentlemen should? Oh yes... I've seen Sir Roger cut men's hands off when he catches them. 'Stops them bearing weapons against us' he says." Gilbert stopped. "You've no need to worry, lad. He'll be right pleased with you."

Josh wasn't so sure but couldn't think of anything useful to say. If he hadn't been taken prisoner by that stupid Henry, he'd have been able to warn his camp and none of the surprise attack would have happened. Now Henry was either dead or a prisoner and he was stuck with the wrong army. At least these two thought he was on their side but he had to escape before he faced Sir Roger. He still couldn't understand why Sir Roger was so angry with him though he remembered a strange dream about him. That dream came from the other time he knew.

Still, his hands were free and he was out of his prison cart. He shook his hands and arms to get the blood flowing again. Pins and needles made them tingle as the feeling returned to his fingers. Gilbert waited by the wagon, a hand on Josh's shoulder.

Now Josh had to wait until the Royalist made a decision or he could work out how to escape. But if he did escape, where could he go? By now he'd be an enemy to both sides. The Parliamentarians thought he'd cost the life of a soldier because he'd warned the enemy. The Royalists would decide he was a traitor when he ran away from his rescuer or when Sir Roger recognised him. Sir Roger must know him or why had he haunted his dreams. He didn't stand a chance whatever he did.

Josh shivered with fright. How could he avoid meeting Sir Roger? If they came face to face something really bad was sure to happen. After all, hadn't Sir Roger's portrait scowled at him. That was when he'd left his familiar world. What would the real live Duke of Bolchester do when they were face to face? He knew they had had nightmare encounters but couldn't remember when nor could he remember his bed...

"Why does the commander want to see me? Why bother with lookouts? That's what they're for... lookouts warn... don't they?"

"Most of the men are well grown. We've not got many lads on the battlefield. Their mothers won't let them join even though the boys want to. Sir Roger's own son is safe at home so that makes you special. What's your name, lad?"

"Josh... er, Joseph, sir." He hoped the soldier hadn't noticed his slip. Josh sounded wrong but again he couldn't work out why.

"Well, you know my name. We'll wait until Linus, that's my mate, gets back."

Josh didn't know what he could do. He had to avoid Sir Roger. His father had told him about Sir Roger before taking him to watch Parliament in action. That was before all the fighting began. His father's words came back to him. "The king wants to tax everyone again because he's spent too much money on himself and his court." Father had begun to explain more. "It should be an interesting debate" but then arguments about the king's expensive tastes had broken out. Josh had watched his father argue with the rest of those Lords who now called themselves Parliamentarians. They'd insisted that the king must go. The country couldn't afford him.

Sir Roger had got very red in the face and puffed himself up to look taller than he was. Then he'd shouted they were all traitors. "The king is the king and no one can challenge him."

There had been more shouting and lots of angry voices and he'd heard his father's voice rise above the others. "The biggest traitor is you and men like you. You claim you are noble but you are too much like the king. You force your tenants, good farmers most of them, to pay you so much rent their children go hungry. You, like the king, spend a fortune on frivolous clothes while your tenants' children go barefoot. They freeze in their homes every winter. You should be ashamed... you and the king."

There'd been a roar of approval from a majority in Parliament and Josh couldn't help himself. He'd shouted with the rest of them and thrown his hat in the air in his excitement. He missed it as it fell and it landed at Sir Roger's feet. The knight picked it up, turned it over in his hands, then looked up to where Josh stood. Josh was speechless. He couldn't move, so powerful was Sir Roger Bolchester's glare. Sir Roger had eyes the colour of a steel sword blade and they cut into his face. Josh had memorised them and would never forget them. He had to avoid Sir Roger.

Gilbert's voice interrupted his thoughts.

"You're very quiet lad. You should be proud of yourself. You'll be treated as a hero. Sir Roger likes those who show initiative. He says too many of the soldiers won't think for themselves. They just wait around until he tells them what to do."

Josh knew why that was. His father had explained, "The Royalists are both greedy and stupid. Those knights who support King Charles waste money on themselves. They feast whenever they get together but they leave their troops to fend for themselves. It's just like the way they treat their tenants. If they are in enemy country, the troops have to fight for any meals they get. It's no wonder most of the country supports Oliver Cromwell."

"Is that why they haven't got proper uniforms like our side," he'd asked his father

"That's right. Lord Cromwell insists that everyone who fights for the Parliamentarians must be paid properly. When he can, he issues good armour and better weapons... and he insists that everyone gets fair rations."

"Then will we win?"

"I'm sure we will. We're fair and the people value that."

But then his father had gone to fight and Josh didn't know where he was. He was frightened he might never see him again. At that memory, he sniffed back a tear. He couldn't show fear. But what could he say to Sir Roger? He was sure Sir Roger would kill him, probably the moment he saw him. He had to think of something.

14

Josh heard the sound of footsteps and a group of bedraggled soldiers approached. He looked at them and decided they didn't deserve to be called Cavaliers. They were much too grimy. He knew the officers wore rich clothes, silks and velvets with lots of fine lace and wide brimmed hats with big feather plumes. Then he remembered his father had dressed like that, especially when he went to Parliament, though his jackets and breeches had been in sombre colours, brown or black or grey. But when he'd gone to fight he'd worn good armour, not like these poor men. He wondered if they'd ever seen the king even though they were part of his Royalist army.

He heard one say, "Only four dead, the rest of us got away. They lost four as well."

"What a waste of our surprise approach. Sir Roger won't be pleased."

"Aye, he told us to raze their camp and not leave a man standing... finish them all off."

"We did our best," a third spoke, "But they were on

guard... and better equipped than us."

"Who's he?" The first soldier spoke again. He pointed at Josh as he questioned Gilbert.

"He'd been captured by them but he managed to warn us about a sentry. Plucky lad."

"Let's go. Sir Roger will want the news."

Josh couldn't tell if that speaker was the officer in charge for he was dressed as shabbily as the rest. He stood straighter and looked more carefully at the men around him. They didn't look like people who dressed well. Some had fresh wounds and he could see blood oozing through the bandage on one man's arm.

Gilbert gave him a nudge and the group started back, retracing their paths. Josh didn't know how far they had to go. He daren't ask either. He was supposed to be one of them. They set off in a straggly line, not at all the disciplined troops he was used to. But he looked no different now. His breeches had been blue but now they were so mud spattered they looked a dull brown and matched the grime on his face.

"Come on, lad. You're not keeping up. You're not injured... are you?"

"I'm alright."

He thought fast. "My head hurts. Those soldiers... the ones who captured me thumped me... hard. I need to rest... just for a short time. You go on, I'll catch you up."

He added the last bit and hoped they would go on without him.

"No lad. If you're not right, someone will stay with you. It's easy to stray off the path and we don't know how close those Roundheads are."

That question was quickly answered. A lookout, scouting ahead, rushed to join the main party. "There's soldiers between us and the main camp."

"We've either got to disperse or find a strategic place. Can we reach those rocks?" The man who seemed to be in charge pointed towards a low cliff.

"We need to keep together," someone muttered.

"Why?" Josh panicked and the troop stared at him as if he'd grown another head.

Gilbert nudged him. "You can get yourself imprisoned if you want. I'm sticking with my mates."

He realised that his own side would treat him as an enemy as long as he was stuck with these Royalists. If he could get away he'd be an enemy to every one except his friend, Captain Harry.

"We'll try and get to the cliff. There's scrub along the base. We can reach our old camp and lie low until they move on. Quietly now!"

As one, the bedraggled bunch stepped off the track and hurried, bent low, towards cover. All the time, Josh watched for a moment when everyone was distracted. If he could get lost he might be able to find a Roundhead troop, perhaps even his father's. If these soldiers caught him again he'd have to pretend the blow to his head had made him fall behind. His head was really hurting but he still watched for the moment he could safely disappear.

They trudged on for about an hour but they were a straggling, disorganised group rather than a troop of fighting men. When they finally arrived at the temporary camp Gilbert dumped his pack and weapon. "I'm off to find the sergeant. Then we'll get your head seen to. There may be food. If we're lucky, the cooks got here safely. They knew some of us would get back late."

Josh breathed freely at last when his friendly guard left him at the edge of the camp. It was still very light and other troops were milling about so he'd have to wait for longer for a chance to escape.

Gilbert reappeared with two bowls of runny stew. "They said it was rabbit... one rabbit doesn't go far for a whole troop."

Josh was so hungry, he didn't care. He gulped down the thin broth and bit greedily into the hard bread that accompanied it.

"Hold on, lad. Break up the bread and drop lumps into the stew. That way, the bread gets soft enough to chew easily and the stew feels quite hearty. Here ... have some salt as well. I always keep a bit about me. Does camp food no end of good."

Josh accepted both the advice and the salt in silence. It did improve the meal but only very slightly. Gilbert grinned at him and made room as Josh curled up on one side, trying to keep warm and immediately fell asleep. He grunted but didn't wake when Gilbert shoved a pack under his head to make him more comfortable.

Three warning whistles from the far side of the camp alerted Gilbert. He struggled to his feet. He looked down at Josh but the boy barely moved when Gilbert shoved him gently with his boot. He left the sleeping boy and answered the call. Something urgent was afoot. They weren't usually called to parade after a hard battle. Josh slept on.

15

Olly and Josh Together

Oliver slid down from the bank where he'd been watching for the returning troops. He was fed up because he'd not been allowed to accompany them and, even in the camp, no one paid attention to him. He knew the surrounding countryside so came and went as he pleased. It was close to his home so he spent his time plotting good places to hide should the Royalists be defeated, though he thought that unlikely. He'd developed the ability to move stealthily. He didn't need that skill in his other life. In that life everyone called him Olly.

He'd found a cave about half way up the low cliff. The entrance was hard to see but he used a hawthorn bush and a mound of tumbled stones as landmarks. It was too small to hide everyone but if they wouldn't let him fight he would look out for himself. He'd torn his clothes in his scramble and tried to brush mud off his black trimmed, red breeches and jacket. Now he looked like

64

the rest of the soldiers, not the son of a prosperous farmer.

It was nearly dark when the stragglers returned. He'd seen they had a boy about his own age in their midst. He tried counting the men but their constant movement confused him. He'd watched as they ate then mustered around Sergeant Tunnard. Then he noticed someone sleeping at the very edge of the camp. So far the only young lad he'd seen was the one brought to the camp with the troops so it must be him. He scrambled down the last scrubby slope and approached the sleeper carefully. If he woke him suddenly he might think he was an enemy and start fighting him.

Oliver crept closer still until he could see that the sleeping boy was dressed in clothing which had once been expensive but was now as drab and dirty as his own. There was something familiar about him. Oliver tried to work out what it was when Joseph turned, perhaps subconsciously aware someone had approached.

Oliver gasped. Joseph had been his best friend before the battles started. He'd not been dirty like that. Why was he treated like a Roundhead. Was Joseph spying... or had he been captured. Should he tell one of the soldiers that there was a spy in the camp?

Joseph felt someone was watching him. He had enough

sense to stay still and listen before he opened one eye a slit. He saw someone kneeling by him, a Royalist boy. Gilbert, a soldier and his guard, wore fustian; coarse, dark brown fabric. This person wore good clothes even though what he could see was torn and dirty.

Oliver sensed the attention. "Joseph... Josh, don't be afraid," he whispered. "It's Oliver, Olly. I'll not hurt you but tell me what you're doing here."

Joseph was appalled at being discovered. Oliver's family was loyal to the king and the boys had not spoken since the war began. Families as well as friends had split over opposing loyalties. What would Oliver do?

"I don't know where I am now. I was scouting the countryside for news of your lot. When I got back, a guard from my Roundhead camp caught me and tied me up. He didn't know me and thought I was a Cavalier spy. He wouldn't let me speak. He tied me up and threw me into a cart."

Oliver gasped. "Go on."

"I untied my feet and the gag but not my hands. Then your lot attacked the camp and thought I was one of them. They rescued me and brought me here. If Sir Roger recognises me... Now I'm everybody's enemy." That was a big speech when he wasn't sure if it was safe to say anything.

"But... but we're not enemies... we're just on opposite

sides..."

Joseph couldn't help grinning at that and after a moment, Oliver did too.

"What are we going to do? We've got to get away."

"I don't know. This is your camp." They looked at each other in silence.

Oliver spoke first. "Well, you can't stay here. You may have been rescued by mistake but someone will work out no one knows you. Then you're done for."

"I have to get away... but you have to stop me. We're stuck whatever I think or do."

There was a long silence as they stared at each other and both thought of clean clothes and showers. Joseph had cramp from his sleep and hadn't stretched yet. He couldn't run if he tried.

Oliver knew he wouldn't give Joseph up to Sergeant Tunnard. The sergeant would skewer Josh with his pike and think nothing of it. Oliver had seen how the sergeant had killed a pig for the Christmas feast. He couldn't let that happen to his friend even if Joseph or Josh was an enemy. He made a decision.

"You'll have to leave but our side has spread out right through the valley. I know where the camps are. I'll have to lead you... if you promise not to give me to the... your lot."

"I'd never do that. Not when you saved me... are we...

can we still be friends?"

"Let's just be friends like we really are and not Roundheads or Cavaliers. I'm Olly, only my mum calls me Oliver." Olly made his decision and waited for Joseph to answer.

The pause went on and on. Finally, Joseph sighed and held out his hand. "I'm still Josh and I'd never not be your friend. I swear I won't give you up. You do the same."

"I swear too." They looked at each other and grinned.

Olly paused as he worked out what had happened.

"The secret panel... I came looking for you..."

"I tripped and fell backwards... But we seem to be stuck in the wrong time. So, what can we do?"

"We'll have to get away from the camp first. Can you walk?"

"I'm not injured. I was just tired."

"We'll need some supplies. I can get us some bread while they're still listening to the sergeant."

"What will you say if you get caught?"

"I'll not get caught. Anyway, my father is their landlord in this time. They have to treat me properly. I'd just get told off for sneaking extra rations." Neither understood how they knew.

Josh watched his friend creep off into the darkness of the camp, not sure yet if he trusted him in spite of him swearing. But if he hid somewhere else and Olly came back with food, they'd never find each other again in the dark. He sighed and took a chance. He'd wait. If they really had been transported to the seventeenth century they'd have to stick together. But how would they return to their own time?

Olly arrived at Josh's side, a bundle in one hand and a stave and a large rag in the other. "We can tie the bread in this and carry it more easily."

It took only a moment and they were ready. They had nothing else to carry and the bread would get lighter as they ate lumps off it. They looked at each other. Olly took a deep breath as he realised what he'd decided to do. Now they were enemies of both sides.

"Come on, this way," and the boys crept away and prepared to follow the line of the hillside.

16

It was strange for Josh to follow but Olly knew this countryside while he wasn't sure. Josh listened to Olly's directions and remembered what a good friend he was.

How did he know that in this time Olly's father worked the next estate to Josh's? Both fathers were farmers but only Josh's was a knight and attended Parliament. When the arguments about the king broke out, Olly's father kept silent. He agreed with Oliver Cromwell's views but thought him misguided. How could Parliamentarians change the way the country was run? When King Charles demanded yet more money in taxes Olly's father had tutted and worried how the tenants, who were already struggling, could pay the higher rents they would be charged.

Josh's father had been outraged. He'd sided with Cromwell straight away. Josh's mother had begged him to be careful. That was the first time Josh had even thought about the way the country was run but decided his father was right. Once more he pictured his father but he saw him watching football. Josh knew the picture was on a television but, again, the image fled.

Because of their differences, their families had stopped talking and meeting so Joseph and Oliver, lifelong friends, had been separated. Now they were together again, beginning another adventure but this time, the adventure was both real and dangerous.

The boys spoke quietly together trying to work out how they'd ended up out of their own time.

"It's weird. I know we don't belong in this time but it's not completely strange. I don't know how I know..." Josh looked helplessly at Olly."

Olly had a memory of another conversation. "In this time my father told me 'If the king didn't waste so much money on his fancy court and expensive jewels he wouldn't need more.' He complained all through one meal time but then he said 'but he is the king and we must always obey him'."

"Sir Roger Bolchester decided that everyone who didn't speak in support of Oliver Cromwell had to be a Royalist like him. He expected everyone loyal to the king to give him money for the war or send their sons to be his soldiers." Josh remembered a conversation. "My father was really angry. Mother kept begging him to be careful." Josh decided his father was right. "I'd have been a Roundhead - a Parliamentarian."

"You are" said Olly quietly.

"That's it. King Charles, the first one, was deposed. Some lords in Parliament imprisoned him and twelve of the lords signed an order for the king to be executed. That was when the Civil War started between those who believed in Cromwell and those who wanted a king back. You must know that too."

"We must have lived back then... well, now... as well as properly. I mean in our own time. It's weird. I don't understand..."

"We'd better go if we're going together."

Josh nodded and they used bushes and rocks to mask their progress as they left the camp.

"Sshhh." Olly signalled to Josh to duck down and stay where he was. He crouched to peer over a low bank then beckoned indicating that all was clear. Their confusion forgotten, they scrambled down the next slope and moved through another empty camp.

The remains of a fire were still just warm. Nearby, they found a flagon of weak beer and shared it between them.

"If there's any bread we'll take it. But hurry."

They scavenged briefly but found nothing else.

"We'll need to move. They could be back soon."

Once again Olly ran ahead and they scrambled up another banking. A thin wedge of moon shone on a distant hillside and the smell of smoke drifted on the breeze.

"We're lucky it's not raining." Josh scanned the sky. "We'd leave tracks anyone could follow."

Olly nodded. His friend was right.

"We need to be careful. There's either another camp or a battle between us and those hills. We need to cross them. We're not very far from my home."

"But will I be safe there?" Josh worried that he'd be taken prisoner.

"Of course. My parents wouldn't harm you."

A shout disturbed their progress. "Hey there. You two." When they looked back, it continued, "Stop! Come here."

"This way," Olly hissed at Josh. He raced towards a patch of scrubby bushes with Josh following.

"Down here." The sounds of shouting speeded them on their way.

Olly whispered, "This place is where my father taught me how to trap rabbits. We had a family feast when I caught my first one."

He sped across familiar ground, racing to where he knew a sunken pathway could help their flight.

"What's this? Where's it go? Josh slid down the steeply sloped bank after him getting yet more mud on the seat of his breeches.

"It's an ancient trackway. Nobody knows how long it's been here. It's older than anybody's memory."

"Which way?"

"Just keep following." Olly hadn't breath for more but he knew where they could scramble up the other side and into the cover of woodland.

Stinging nettles lashed at their legs and brambles scratched at their sleeves trying to hold them back. Wild garlic, crushed under their feet, scented a damp stretch of the path.

Josh's chest was bursting when Olly gasped, "Here..." He pointed and Josh stopped but bent over panting. "Come on, Josh. Quickly. Listen."

They heard men's voices and the sounds of twigs breaking underfoot were coming closer. The bank was steep but Olly clawed his way up using tussocks of grass for footholds. Josh saw how he did it and followed. There was a steeper lip at the top which the boys fell over almost together.

"The trees..." Olly pointed and they scrambled upright again and ran the last few metres into a thicket.

Dense shrubs were interspersed with spindly branches; birch, hawthorn and hazel bushes with brambles tangling everything. Further in, they saw taller trees, oak and ash.

"They've not got dogs. We can slow down a bit." Josh was puffed.

"No, they'll find traces where we've been. There's a good tree we can climb."

Josh really needed to rest but his friend hurried on. He followed more slowly, trying to control his panting, until they could see an enormous horse chestnut tree. Its leaves still clung to the branches, gold and red and brown.

Olly stopped at its base. Josh caught up and Olly pointed to a low branch.

"Jump. You can reach that and then pull yourself up. Quick."

This time in their friendship, Olly was the strong leader. When Josh managed to grasp the branch, Olly grabbed his legs and heaved him up.

"Now get that higher branch and pull yourself up."

As soon as there was space and Josh straddled a branch Olly followed. He jumped, clasped both arms round the branch and swung his legs up, secure once he'd locked them over the wood.

"Get a move on. Up there... they're getting nearer."

Josh climbed and was half way up the trunk as Olly climbed rapidly after him and whispered, "Find a solid branch and move along it. Then lie flat on it."

Once Josh was safe, Olly chose his own branch and stretched out along it too. He hooked his feet over smaller boughs and wrapped his arms around the branch as if cuddling it.

"They must have come this way. Their tracks were so

clear... easy to follow. Better look up into those trees."

"Wait for the others, they're just behind us..."

"Okay. You search those trees, I'll start here."

Both Josh and Olly held their breath, afraid if the leaves stirred they'd be discovered. That's when Josh felt an insect crawling on his leg. He couldn't stand the tickle. He tried to flick it off. His foot snagged a tiny twig which snapped off and fell, stirring leaves and other small branches on its way.

"You hear that?"

The second soldier peered up, searching the branches then picked up a pebble and pitched that towards Josh's branch. A bird fluttered out and its indignant twittering set birds on other branches complaining too.

"Well, they're not up there! Come on. Keep up, you lot. Let's move on."

Josh and Olly let out careful breaths. The soldiers chasing them were baffled. Olly had guessed correctly. Though the soldiers peered up the trunks of the larger trees, Olly and Josh were out of their sight. The soldiers didn't bother to scan along the branches and Olly had made certain that they were high up and well hidden by leaves. They stayed put for a long time.

Eventually Josh asked, "Can we get down yet?"

"Not yet,"Olly hissed. "They'll have to come back this way."

They heard the grumbling and voices carried to them on the wind. Then the noise of twigs snapping underfoot and leaves rustling got louder until the small troop crashed by underneath them and disappeared the way they'd come.

They waited in the tree top until the natural woodland noises resumed and the alarm calls of the birds gave way to a gentle twittering.

Once again Olly warned, "Be careful, Josh. Go slowly and carefully. The birds could still give us away."

"Alright."

Olly heard his whispered agreement and shuffling noises as Josh began his climb down. He followed, picking his way from branch to branch until he too could drop to the ground.

"Is it safe now?" Josh asked.

"More than that. I think we're proper partners now," and he held out his hand for Josh to shake.

When they set off again the going was easier but Olly was still worried. "I think there'll be guards at my home... unless it's been captured by Roundheads."

"We're not all Roundheads. Roundheads are just those London boys. We're Parliamentarians," Josh argued.

"You've still got short hair," countered Olly. "But shush. We've still got to be careful."

Olly took the lead again. Now he was on familiar

ground. He knew the little hidden routes that would take them home to safety.

17

Once they were sure their pursuers had given up, Olly and Josh set off running whenever the ground was smooth enough and there was cover from trees and hedges. But they slowed as the boys neared Olly's home, Garfield House.

"If my father has posted guards, they may not recognise me... especially looking like this." Olly indicated the mud on his clothes and his knees peeking through torn breeches. Josh looked even dirtier. "You look like a town boy escaped from an apprentice master," he added as he looked Josh up and down.

Josh grinned at him though with all the dirt on his face, it could have been a scowl. "We'll have to creep closer... see if it's safe. If you know the guards, we'll be all right..."

"Yes... well... We'll go and look." Olly didn't sound happy. "There's the wall," he whispered, pointing ahead. "There's a small postern gate round there." Olly pointed to where the wall curved away from them. "It's used by the farm workers on rent days... there's a path to the kitchens."

Josh had forgotten about that small entrance.

The boys used whatever cover they found while still keeping the wall in sight. When they saw a head above the wall, they dropped to the ground and made themselves as flat as possible. The face looked all around then shouted, "There's no one there. You're hearing things," and disappeared again.

Still lying flat, they looked at each other. "What made him look?"

"We were really quiet. It couldn't have been us." Josh was as anxious as his friend. He was also even more tired and his head ached. "I need a drink.'

"The well has pure water. If we can get into the inner courtyard we should find the bucket full."

Josh nodded but slowly. They crept closer to the wall where it curved away then stopped as shouts and sounds of arguing reached them.

"What shall we do?"

"I need to know if my father and mother are all right. Are they here or has the house been captured. I'm going to look..."

"No!" Josh shivered. It didn't matter who was in the house, they needed to stick together.

Olly hesitated. "Well, if my family is being attacked, it's your side doing it... but if the Roundheads have arrived, I can ask to be taken to my father even if I'm taken prisoner first."

Josh gasped. His mouth opened but no words came.

"It's all right. I don't intend to get captured. I'll be really careful."

Josh still looked doubtful. "And if my father's men are successful?"

"I'm not going to get captured. Stop worrying." Olly sounded more confident than he felt. His heart thumped as he crept closer to the wall and the narrow gate.

When he had slithered round the curve in the wall he was lost from sight, Josh heard barking in the distance. He hoped Olly was not the cause. Olly would always be his friend, even though their families were no longer friendly. If the dogs were after Olly, would they find him too?

Josh lay in the grass and waited and hoped. He didn't know how long he lay there but suddenly a hand grabbed his shoulder. He opened his mouth but a hand clapped over it before a sound emerged.

"Shh. It's me. I think it's your lot but I can't see any of your family. I think it's two troops and they're squabbling over stores. They're so busy fighting each other, they didn't take any notice of me."

As the hand was removed, Josh rolled over to look at his friend. He gasped when he saw what he carried.

"You've got bread.'

"And water." Olly grinned as he pulled a leather flagon from behind his back. "I saw a soldier fill it and sneaked it when he went to help a mate."

They split the bread and took turns drinking from the flagon. They had not known when they'd next find food. They were so relieved that they forgot to stay low.

Large hands grabbed their collars and yanked them to their feet. "I told you I heard something. Then I spotted that ragamuffin pinching food. Got you. You'll have some explaining to do."

18

The boys stared at each other. Now what? Neither recognised the soldiers. Nor could they tell if they were Roundheads or Cavaliers for their clothes were torn and dirty and nearly as ragged as their own.

Josh spoke first. "Who are you? Where are you taking us? We're hungry... just looking for food."

"Orphans, eh! It's dangerous to roam around in the country on your own." A second soldier commented.

Olly opened his mouth but Josh kicked him before he could speak. He glared at Josh then realised that being orphans could keep them safe, at least if no one recognised them.

"This way, lads."

The first soldier nodded at his companion and the soldiers each took a boy by an arm and marched them through the gates. Olly looked all round, anxious to see if his father's servants or tenants were around. 'If I'm recognised, everything should be all right,' he thought. Josh looked to see if he could find a Roundhead uniform so he could ask after his father.

They soon realised that Olly's family and servants had gone and his home looked as if it had been looted. As they were led up the stairs and through what had been the main family room, Olly saw his mother's favourite jug broken on the floor. One of the captors kicked pieces out of the way and a sharp edge gouged a groove in what had been a polished floor.

Josh nudged his friend and put a hasty finger to his lips to indicate 'Don't say anything'.

He looked around and then asked, in a voice that sounded braver than he felt "Whose house is this?"

A harsh voice answered "It's mine now" and Josh saw Sir Roger Bolchester step into view.

"I shall use the land to add to my estates. The stones from this house will be used in my castle. When I catch the people from this farm those I don't execute will become my farm hands."

Olly gulped. Josh stepped sideways onto his foot.

"Ow!"

"I'm sorry." Josh spoke loudly then mouthed "Don't say anything..."

Olly hopped up and down clutching his foot but his nod told Josh he understood.

"I've seen you before." Sir Roger looked hard at Josh. He sensed something was up but didn't know what. "If you two are spies, I'll soon get it out of you. I'll not let you free to cause trouble for my men. My soldiers are important."

Josh heard a quiet 'Hmm' from behind which changed to a cough when Sir Roger glanced around. His soldiers weren't as well looked after as Sir Roger pretended. Josh wondered if and how they could use that information.

"What shall I do with them, Sir Roger?"

"Lock them in that small attic for now. I'll decide later..."

Someone pushed the boys forward again and frog-marched up the grand, carved wood of the main staircase. They were pushed along a corridor to a servants' door. Behind it, narrow stone steps led up to the attics. The soldiers shoved the boys upwards then along a low and even narrower passageway under the highest point of the roof. Doors, open on both sides, showed servants quarters and box rooms. A door at the end led into a tiny space. They saw a small window set at knee height and eaves that sloped down to its top so that the room was narrow and dark. It was unfurnished apart from an old chest pushed against one wall.

"There's only old fabrics in there... use them to sleep on."

"We're hungry," Josh interrupted. He crossed his fingers behind his back to stop Olly blurting out that it wasn't true but Olly caught on.

"...and thirsty." Olly pleaded.

Olly really did feel hungry again and so helpless that a tear rolled down his cheek. He saw Josh looking and felt ashamed as well as helpless. His friend didn't need a baby for a companion.

"Me, too," said Josh in a very small voice.

The soldiers looked at each other, undecided. "We've not got much... very poor rations."

He shut up when his companion dug him in the ribs to keep the troop's plight secret but seeing the looks on their faces, the second one offered, "We'll see what we can do," and they closed the door.

The lock clicked with a very final sound.

19

Josh and Olly looked at each other, not sure what to do or say. There wasn't much to explore. The room was tiny and, because it was half under the slope of the roof, seemed smaller.

Josh paced the room then peered out of the window. Away in the distance he could see the flag on the tower of Bolchester Castle fluttering in the wind. His father's land was in the opposite direction. He hoped his home had not suffered as Olly's had.

They both heard the footsteps clumping up the stairs and sat down with their backs against the corridor wall where the ceiling was highest.

The soldier who had first caught them unlocked the door and checked to see where they were. They stayed still and waited. He said nothing, just nodded at them and put a lump of hard bread and a jug of liquid on the floor at his feet. He nodded at them again, backed out of the room and locked the door once more.

They heard his footsteps clumping away and disappearing into the distance. They were still hungry as

Josh broke the lump in two. Even though the bread was really old, they started to chew lumps off.

Olly peered into the jug. "If it's from the well, it's clean water. It will be safe to drink." He took a long sniff at it then drank from one side. "That's good."

He passed the jug to Josh who also drank. Between them they finished the scrap meal and leaned back against the wall.

It had been early morning when they'd been captured. Now the light was fading once more.

Olly crawled to the window. "There's dark clouds. I think there's going to be a storm."

"Well we're dry here and it's warmer than out there."

Olly looked at his friend. "But it's our chance to escape. They'll not bother too much if there's bad weather... not when they're so poorly provided for. You saw their clothes... We can try for your home. We both know where we are."

Josh still said nothing. Olly turned back to the window and began to tug at it. It rattled in its frame though the catch was rusted tight. He took off a shoe and banged at the catch then tried it again.

It was looser this time but still stuck. It took a couple more knocks before he unlatched it. Then he had to work at the frame which had swollen onto the wood. At last the window flew open and a gust of cold air swirled about him. He leaned out and saw a buttress jutting out below. It was two bricks wide and was capped with flat stones. He saw it sloped down to the roof of an outhouse and the outhouse roof stretched almost to the outer wall.

"Josh, I've got a plan."

Those weren't the most comforting words Josh heard. Josh was sleepy. The poor food and difficult previous night had exhausted him.

"Do we have to use it now?"

"Yes. We may never get another chance. Come and see."

Olly pointed out their escape route. "The difficult bit will be staying on the buttress... we've got to drop onto it. After that, it should be easy."

Josh decided that sounded too good to be true.

Olly eased his feet and legs over the window ledge and wriggled to the edge. "I'm going to turn round to face the wall before I let go," he said and disappeared.

Josh gasped. It was all too sudden, too fast. But he daren't think what would happen if he was left behind. What would the soldiers do? He took a deep breath and struggled on to the window ledge.

Olly stepped gingerly a short distance from the house wall, turned and sat down astride the buttress. It was quite a stretch but he managed to get a grip with his knees.

He looked up at Josh wavering on the ledge above him. "Let yourself down facing the wall. Hang on to the window ledge until you feel steady. Make sure you're level with me... and this wall."

He waited while Josh manoeuvered himself to the edge. "Can you turn round?"

"Yes."

"You've got to let yourself hang. Hold tight to the window ledge."

"I'm stuck. What do I do now?" Josh sounded terrified.

"Keep still. Then, when you're ready, you're going to let go. Keep your feet together and you'll land by me."

Josh clung on, not able to climb back and not daring to let go.

"You can let go now. I'll catch you. You can't fall off." Olly hoped that was true.

"I'm coming." Josh let go at the same moment.

As his feet hit the brickwork he started to slip. Olly grabbed at his clothes, pulled until he had a large handful, and hauled Josh safely onto the top of the buttress. He kept hold of him until Josh stopped shaking.

"I'm all right now... I think."

Olly laughed in relief. "I'm sure that's the most difficult bit. We can crawl along to that roof now. We'll work out what to do then. Can you turn round now and face that way?"

"Yes. I'm okay."

Olly waited until Josh was facing the outer wall like him, ready to grab again if he looked unsteady. Then he swivelled round until he could see the outhouse. Caterpillar-like, the boys inched along the buttress trying not to scrape their knees or tear their clothes more on the uneven stonework. They were lucky, the courtyards were empty on both sides and though kitchen sounds came from one direction, no one appeared nor noticed their progress.

The outhouse roof had a shallow slope of stone slabs with only a narrow gap between it and their wall walk. When Olly sat on the end and stretched out his legs he could just reach the roof. He pushed himself over the gap and found he could stand quite easily. Josh soon followed, more confident this time though he still grabbed Olly's hand for security. Together they crossed the roof. There was a narrow passage at the far end. This ran between the outhouse and the outer wall. This wall was higher than their foothold on the roof.

"I know what we can do." Olly tugged at Josh's sleeve as Josh looked at the height of the wall. "It's not far to the ground. We've got to get off this roof. There's another postern... the watchman's gate just round that building. It's barred, not locked."

Josh just nodded and looked for the best way off the roof. Olly nudged him again and pointed. A wooden gutter ended in a spout over a water barrel. It was close to the wall but in sight of the house windows.

"No one's seen us. We could go that way then hide in this passageway."

Josh nodded and slid to the edge of the roof, turned to face it and dropped over the edge, hanging on as best he could.

"You're right over the barrel." Olly's whisper helped him and Josh let go and hoped the lid would hold. As soon as he was steady he dropped to the ground to wait for Olly.

"I'm coming." Olly followed, rolling off the barrel and falling at Josh's feet. He brushed himself down and Olly rubbed his knee where he'd landed. "I'm all right... this way now."

At the edge of the passage, Olly checked the courtyard, put a finger to his lips and gestured Josh to follow.

They crept beside the wall for what seemed ages before reaching the postern gate that Olly knew. A hefty wooden bar was pushed through iron hoops on both sides. It needed both boys pulling and pushing to free the door. They leaned the bar soundlessly against the wall then Olly pushed at the iron latch. It stuck. He pushed harder and it lifted with a clang as iron hit iron. They looked round fearfully.

"Quick."

They struggled to open the door. It was both heavy and stiff.

"We've got to close it... not give ourselves away..."

Josh nodded and they pulled the gate closed then looked around. They'd escaped. They were out but they still had two big problems - could they stay free and which way should they go?

20

Once they were well away from the wall and their prison they hid in a stand of birch trees. Josh looked back and could just see their prison window in the distance. He turned to face the same way he had at the attic window and pointed.

"Bolchester Castle is that way in the east so this is the way to my home. I know the direction from here but I don't know if the paths are safe. We need to keep off paths and tracks. We might get caught again."

Olly nodded agreement.

"But a track could guide us the right way. Let's get away from here. We can decide from the other side of the estate."

They agreed which way they'd go and scurried away from Olly's one-time family home, keeping low and using any cover they could find.

They emerged on sloping land with a stony cart track leading toward Josh's home. They stayed above it but followed its line and only straightened up when they could no longer see any part of Olly's house, not even a chimney. By then the sun was low in the sky and, though filtered by a growing mist, shone directly into their eyes, blinding them to an early view of anyone moving on the road. As the sun dropped further, a mist thickened. It got colder.

Olly shivered. "I'm hungry again."

"So am I but I don't know what we can do about it until we get to my home." Josh just hoped his hadn't suffered the same fate as Olly's. The soldiers squabbling there didn't look as if they belonged to any army.

Olly voiced Josh's thoughts. "If it's still your house... If it's not been captured too." He wasn't optimistic.

The sun soon dropped completely and the boys began to run. They needed to use what light was left and they'd less than an hour until it was completely dark.

"I know that wood." Josh stopped and pointed to a stretch of trees cutting across the land.

The cart track ran through the wood disappearing into the darkness under the branches. "There's charcoal burners and hermits live there. They don't like strangers much."

"Are you a stranger? Will they recognise you?" Olly asked.

"I don't know. I was always forbidden to go there after dark. Father told me dangerous outlaws hid there as well as the charcoal burners." Josh felt nervous again.

"So what are we going to do?"

"I don't know... if we're really quiet... maybe we could creep through."

"Can we keep near the road? So we don't get lost?"

The sky darkened. The woodland looked darker still. The boys crept towards the cart track below them, showing black silhouettes against the sky.

They didn't know they were already being observed but felt uneasy as they approached the dark trees. The watchers noted their progress and wondered what to do about them.

"Can we go round?" Olly voiced Josh's fears.

"That wood goes on for miles. It's too far... it's a long way just going through and there's more chance of meeting soldiers in the open." He tried to convince himself but both boys slowed.

They reached the edge of the shadow cast by the trees as the light finally disappeared.

"We've nowhere else to go. If my home's been captured like yours we'll both be outlaws. Come on." Josh tried to sound brave.

He led the way leaving the hillside but still staying away from the track. As they entered the trees it became more difficult to see the path but they knew that if they lost it, they'd go round in circles. The wood gave no clues in the dark.

An owl hooted and something rustled in the undergrowth. Olly grabbed at Josh's arm.

"It's only an animal." Josh whispered. "Keep close."

Another hoot sounded, closer this time, followed by an answering call.

"That's not a real owl. Someone's watching us." Olly squealed. "How can we pass by them?"

"Shh... I think... We need to send them to the wrong place. Keep still." Josh bent and felt the ground around his feet.

A third hoot sounded and again the boys heard answering calls. Josh straightened up slowly, twisted without moving his feet so that he could just make out the lighter pattern of the track and threw a small stone. It scattered several pebbles as it landed. Josh waited a moment and threw a second, this time harder. Again the rustling noise sounded but this time further away. He waited longer before pitching the third stone. Olly thought his chest would burst, he daren't breathe.

This time they heard the scuffling from further away. Josh gripped Olly's arm pulling him close. "I think they're following that noise. I think we can move but be very careful where you put your feet. I'll go first."

Josh crept forward testing each spot before he put any weight on his foot. He sensed Olly following him though Olly was silent too.

They continued through the trees, stopping every few minutes to listen for movement, voices or strange bird calls. It was hard to tell how long they'd been creeping through the trees, or how far they'd travelled. They stopped every few metres to listen. They heard one owl call in the distance and very nearly screamed in fright when a white phantom swooped over them. Olly clutched at Josh.

"That's a barn owl, a real one. It's hunting." Josh sounded more confident. "It's all right."

They tiptoed on, stopping every time they heard rustling in the undergrowth until one or other realised it was just a small animal.

"An outlaw would be a lot louder than that." Josh tried to reassure himself as much as his companion.

They didn't know how long they had been tiptoeing through the wood but it never seemed to end.

A sharp crack rang out. It sounded like a musket shot. Josh had missed his footing. He'd landed on the end of a rotten branch. The boys knew the sound of it breaking would bring their woodland pursuers running.

"Under those bushes" Josh tugged at Olly and the boys hid rapidly but silently. Olly was sure the sound of their heartbeats could be heard for miles. They lay motionless for what seemed like hours but was only five minutes. They heard nothing but the normal woodland sounds.

At last Josh poked Olly, "Let's move. I think it's clear."

They shuffled out from under the bushes and, very carefully, very slowly stood up, then waited when they were upright. There were still no suspicious sounds. Josh gave a quick tug at Olly's arm and led the way again. This time he checked every single pace. They'd no idea how long their woodland ordeal had lasted.

Olly tapped Josh's shoulder and whispered in his ear "Is that a clearing? Do you know where we are?"

Josh looked about and took a deep breath. "I think the trees are thinning. I think we're nearly through. Don't talk yet... Careful."

The boys continued to check each piece of ground before stepping onwards. At the edge of the trees, Josh pulled Olly against the gnarled and bumpy trunk of an ancient oak. They stood there gathering their breath and their courage, using starlight to plot a way ahead.

"I think we should run until we can hide again."

"But we'll be seen."

"Right... there's a dip in the land... see that humpy bit of grass?" He waited for Olly to nod. "There's a hollow beyond it. We'll make for there and drop flat again."

Josh waited to feel Olly's nod, patted his shoulder and pelted out onto the open, then over the hillock and dropped flat out of sight. Olly landed on top of him, rolled off and breathed a big sigh of relief.

21

They lay panting in the hollow hardly able to believe they'd got through the wood without more danger.

"We're not safe yet." Josh knew what Olly was thinking. "We've still got to reach my house."

"What if it's been captured? What will we do?"

"I don't know. I don't want to think about it. If father has gone... or been taken prisoner... or..." Josh stopped.

What if his father was dead? For the first time since the attic he felt tears ready to fall. He sniffed, hard. He thought he had to be strong for Olly. Didn't Olly depend on him?

Olly read his thoughts. He'd had the same worries. He'd not seen any of his own family or servants before they'd been imprisoned in his home.

"If father's there, we're safe." Josh worked things out. "But if he's not, my family might know where father's gone... or where we can find Captain Harry... but what do we do if there are more Royalists?"

Olly nearly laughed aloud. "That's another long speech... but we'll have to be really careful until we know for sure." He peered over the edge of the hollow. "I can't see anyone. Shall we go on?"

"All right. But let's take care." Josh still wasn't very happy but knew they had to move.

"Ready?"

"Yes," said Olly.

Together they rose to their feet and set off. They were cold from the night in the trees. Their clothes were damp from lying in the hollow and a breeze chilled their backs.

"I'm tired. Is it far?" Olly shivered.

Josh grunted. He was tired too. "I don't think it's too far but..." he didn't finish.

"Can't we use the cart track?"

Again there was no proper answer from Josh. He usually told Olly what to do but right now, he didn't have any answers. He was frightened his home had also been captured.

As they trudged on, the sun began to rise behind them but it was still too low to warm them up. Neither spoke. After two miles, which felt like ten, Josh spied the top of his chimney pots.

"If we go much further we'll be seen... doesn't matter who's there... sentries will raise the alarm."

"So, what do we do now?" Olly asked.

"I don't know." Josh snapped. He was too tired to make

a plan. Then he remembered, "Yes, I do. If we go that way," he pointed to his right, away from the track, "we'll come to a shepherd's shelter. We'll go there."

"And sleep?"

"Okay."

They had a plan. They reached the rough hut without seeing anyone else. Josh looked around for sheep or the shepherd but there was no one around. The hut was empty. "The sheep must have been moved to some other field to graze."

They ran the last few metres and Olly pulled open the door. A stale smell greeted them for the place was empty and unused. It was tiny with rough wattle walls and a straw thatch for the roof. By the reek, the rain leaked in but now the day was clear and the sun was higher, beginning to warm the land.

An untidy pile of straw filled one corner. Together, the boys pulled it over the floor, pulled the door almost shut, and collapsed onto their makeshift bed. Within a minute, both boys were sleeping, unaware of how much time passed.

It was light when Olly woke and stretched. Josh slept on. Olly pushed the door enough to peer around and look for people. He needed to pee, he was bursting. He had to get outside soon. He took a chance, crawled round the side of the hut and away from the doorway.

He finished and was buttoning up his breeches when Josh joined him.

"I heard you. My turn."

When he too was comfortable he grinned at Olly, "What next? Search for food or try for home?"

"I don't know. What time is it?"

The sky was cloudy but the sun was shining above the horizon in the direction they'd come. Olly gasped at the sky and Josh grinned.

"I think we slept through half a day and all night. I think it's the next day... or do I mean tomorrow?"

They moved back towards the doorway, grinning at each other. Sleep had revived them. The long night in the hut had dried them. Though they were hungry they felt more cheerful. They were ready for whatever came next.

22

They began to walk, still keeping away from the cart track.

"Maybe everybody has left your home. Where would they go?"

Josh didn't answer, just walked faster. Olly hurried to keep up.

By now the house was in clear view but there was no smoke coming from the chimneys.

"What if...?" Olly stopped abruptly, chilled by his thought.

"What if they're all dead? I don't know," and Josh walked even faster, no longer cautious.

Within minutes they were in sight of the windows. All were closed but the day was still early so that was not unusual. They got closer and Josh stopped and pointed away from the track.

"See that gate?"

Olly followed Josh's finger and nodded. He didn't know what he was supposed to say.

"There, it's not in sight of the main rooms. Ready?

We'll run for it."

"The dogs should be barking," Josh muttered as they reached the gateway.

Olly glanced at his worried face. "Are we going in?"

"I have to. You can wait here while I find out."

"No. I'm sticking with you."

Josh grasped the iron door handle and twisted it. They heard the latch move and Josh pushed gently. He opened the door just far enough to see a little of the pathway beyond. There was still no one in sight.

"I'm going."

"All right. I'm coming too."

The door scraped against the inner path but no one appeared to investigate the noise. Josh led the way round the building to the kitchen door.

The kennels were empty. The hens had gone. He ignored outhouses and sheds for the only noise was their own. They entered the kitchen. No one. The scullery was bare. There were no sounds suggesting the company of other people.

Josh said nothing.

Olly watched his face. Now his friend was suffering the same worries he'd had though it was different here. At his home, they'd been caught early while they explored. Olly had not known if his parents were still there or if they'd escaped, but there had been people about. That place bustled with soldiers although they'd not seen very much before they were locked in the attic.

Here, everything was silent. It was the silence of abandonment. Had everyone run away, escaped when war and trouble drew near? Or had Josh's parents and all the people belonging to the house and grounds been taken prisoner and marched away? Maybe they were dead... Olly pushed that thought away. Whatever must Josh be thinking?

"We should look for people... search for clues... we can't just stand here." Olly shook Josh's arm but only very gently. He'd never seen his friend with such a blank face and nothing to say.

Josh turned to him. Olly shivered. Josh's eyes stared straight through him. Olly had never seen empty eyes like that though his father had described the face of one of the farm workers when he'd nearly cut his foot off with a scythe. Was Josh in the same sort of state? Olly made another decision.

He took Josh's arm again. "We'll go through the whole house. We'll be very quiet in case people are waiting to attack us. They may all be hiding."

He didn't think that was true but he had to get Josh moving. "Come on. Where's the best place to start? Are there pantries and store cupboards by the kitchen?"

Josh still looked blank but at least he nodded. He

waved a hand in the direction of a doorway in a darker corner of the room. Olly took his arm. He led Josh to the door then tried to get his mind working again. "Is this a pantry or just a cupboard?"

"What? What did you say? Why have you pushed me over here?"

Olly heaved a sigh. "Are you all right? We're going to search the house. We may at least find some food." His stomach rumbled to remind them both they were hungry.

"It's the pantry. The meat pantry." Josh turned the handle and opened the door.

A squeal panicked them and a large cat sprang out of the space, its black fur standing out giving it a wild, demented look.

"That's one of the mousers. What's it doing in the meat store?" Josh looked after the animal as it raced out of the kitchen.

The cold pantry was empty. A large oval platter showed bloody traces where a joint of meat had been. The store had been emptied. A wire gauze fronted cupboard on the top shelf, just within their reach, was also empty.

"There's a cold store through there," Josh led the way back into the kitchen and to a narrow door which opened onto a confined space lined with shelves on both sides. Once again it had been cleared of any provisions.

"There's still the dry store and the vegetable store in the cellar with the beer and wine."

Josh led the way and Olly was relieved that he seemed to be more like the friend he knew. He hoped it would last.

The vegetable cellar seemed as empty as the other stores. Olly lifted every earthenware cooler and shook every sack. He'd almost given up when one sack sagged with its contents. Treasure? Olly had found three apples.

They gnawed into one each then searched a kitchen drawer for knives and shared the third. They were still hungry.

Olly nudged Josh. "We need to search the rest of the house. Come on."

Josh said nothing, staring at the empty shelves and broken dishes on the floor at his feet.

"That one was my mother's special dish." He picked up a piece.

"Leave it. Let's see if your mother's left a message." Olly tugged at his arm.

Josh looked at him. "You never saw your parents. We never even knew if they were still there..."

"Come on, let's search the house."

This time Josh followed him and together they entered the dining room. The table was bare of food and plates were pushed back and abandoned. Chairs were left as if people had jumped up and rushed out.

Josh saw that the ornate, silver candlestick holder which usually sat in the middle was missing as was most of the cutlery. The silver tureen had vanished from the sideboard but the room still looked as if it expected people back at any moment.

Josh walked out and across the hall. Pictures still hung where they always had but the floor showed mud and scuff marks instead of its usual polish. The sitting room was unchanged. Just empty.

They crept up the wide staircase, the only sounds the creak of wood as they stepped higher. Still without speaking, they toured the bedrooms. The beds were left as if sleepers had just climbed out of them. In three rooms, clothes were strewn across the floor.

Josh stopped at one door. "This was my room." It looked the same as the others. Josh picked up breeches, "These were my second best pair."

Just for a moment, the shock of the destruction had left Josh upset and speechless.

"Why not put them on now. They're clean." Olly picked up other garments. "You can have fresh clothes. You'll feel better."

"So can you. Find some things that fit, we're nearly the same height."

When Olly glanced sideways at him he was relieved to see Josh sorting other clothes. Josh found brown breeches, looked at Olly who nodded and took the clothes Josh handed to him.

They left their bedraggled garments on the floor and faced each other, tired and hungry but feeling better than they had in a long time.

"I'm all right. It's such a shock..."

"I know." Olly nodded. "What now?"

"We'd better check the attics," Josh was thinking ahead again.

23

Olly let Josh carry on planning. He didn't like making all the decisions so was glad when Josh led the way to the attic stairs, narrow stone ones similar to those they'd been forced up in Olly's home.

Most of the attic rooms were empty. The servants had gone and it looked as if they'd taken all their belongings and their bedding with them.

In the last room, bigger than their prison, but under the eaves, there was more evidence of hurry. Drag marks in the dust on the floor showed where a heavy chest had been pulled into the light.

Josh saw Olly's face. "It's all right. I think it only had old clothes and broken toys. We'd no hidden treasure and special hiding places."

But Josh was wrong.

"What's that?" Olly pointed to a tiny slot in the woodwork under the steepest part of the sloping roof where it continued down to the low wall on that edge of the room. They saw how the chest had hidden it but the tiny slot was still hard to see.

Josh knelt to examine the hole. He couldn't even get his finger nail in. Without a word, Olly unbuckled his breeches and passed the belt to Josh.

Josh looked surprised but used the metal edge as a lever. A small doorway opened easily.

The boys looked closely. The door had been well disguised so the edges were impossible to see when the panels were closed. It fitted exactly against two wooden beams which formed part of the roof support. They peered into the opening.

A narrow space ran under the eaves and behind the supporting wall. It was large enough for someone to crawl along if they were careful but seemed to reach a dead end where the eaves met the corner of the house.

"Well no one's hiding there. It doesn't look very useful. I suppose it was space for treasure if we'd had any."

Olly nodded.

"We can't stay here. We need food. There's none left here. I hope my parents left and weren't..." Josh left the frightening bit unsaid.

"This Captain Harry...?"

"He was known to my father," Josh answered. "My father thought well of him. I wonder where he is?"

The two friends backed away from the hidden place. "We'll carry on looking." said Josh.

Olly closed the panel and checked it was invisible

before he nodded and they went down the stairs together and through the hall to the kitchen door.

Josh ran back into the dining room. Olly waited not sure what to do but Josh soon reappeared. This time he carried a pottery jug and two kitchen knives he'd found.

"We can use this for water... and if we find something to eat..."

Olly still said nothing though he took the knife Josh offered and stuffed it down his stocking.

Josh drew water from the kitchen barrel and both boys drank before Josh refilled the jug and they set off.

It was still quiet outside but the day was well on. The sun had passed overhead and was beginning to drop towards the west.

"Let's keep going west. That way we'll follow the light..." He glanced at Josh and continued, "and we haven't seen anyone between our homes."

"Good idea, Olly. Maybe we'll find my parents with Captain Harry."

Olly said nothing but started walking away with Josh beside him.

24

They walked for some time but saw no one. The countryside appeared empty of people although they passed cows grazing peacefully. Someone must be looking after them.

After a while they saw traces of a battle. It didn't cover a large area but fences were down and the ground churned up. Olly picked up a pike handle, broken about half way. There was no sign of the dangerous metal end but he decided it might be useful. They travelled further until the light began to fade again.

This time Josh decided. "We'll find a haystack and dig a hole where we can hide until the morning... and maybe stay warm"

He looked at Olly, thinking he might argue, but Olly nodded his agreement. The worries of the day had tired them both.

Quite soon they found what they needed, an untidy haystack that looked as if fighting had carried on around it. Olly picked up a broken arrow to add to his armoury. Josh looked at it, pulled a face but said nothing.

They found a place where the stack was partly fallen and dragged out a bundle of corn stooks to make a cave. Olly used his pike handle to hold up their roof. It would be a disaster if the stack collapsed on them. Josh kicked at the sides and pulled loose straw from the bundles. They shared the last of the water and crept into their hiding place then dragged loose straw around the hole to hide it.

When they next stirred, it was past daybreak and birds were twittering.

They shivered as they clambered out of their temporary bed and stretched in the early morning air.

Suddenly Josh stiffened. He clutched at Olly. "Listen."

Hoof beats approached and slowed. They scrambled back into their home made cave, again using loose straw to disguise the opening. They heard the horse stop and the rider dismount and pat his animal.

"There, boy. It's just a friend," the rider reassured his mount as hoof beats of a second horse approached, this time from a different direction. That rider stopped and dismounted.

The boys wondered if they were going to be stuck while more troops gathered. They daren't poke a hole to watch because rustling straw could give them away. They hardly dared to breathe. Were the soldiers Parliamentarians or Royalists? Either way, they weren't safe if they were discovered.

"Luke saw those dratted boys around here.'

"They must be spying..."

They couldn't hear much. The straw muffled the voices and the horses' bridles rattled and tinkled when they lowered their heads to graze but then they heard, "We need to find them. It's important. They'll have to..." The rest was lost in the sound of the horses snorting.

When the animals settled again, they heard, "Yes. Someone's for it... serve them right. Those stupid boys... running off. I know what I'd do."

"Well, we need to catch them first."

Josh and Olly tried but couldn't hear more until, "We're going to rendezvous at Bankhouse Hall. Captain Harry sent word. We can use it as our HQ while we rally. Tell your company and we'll meet there at noon tomorrow."

Josh gulped and Olly held his breath in case Josh gasped at the news.

There were more instructions but spoken too quietly for the boys to hear properly and anyway, Josh was filled with the wild hope his parents might be safe.

They heard the sound of the horses fading as the men galloped away with their message.

Once they felt safe again, Olly let out a breath. "Is it back to your home then?"

"We'll have to go back. Captain Harry will help us... my

parents must be all right."

They crawled out of the stack again and looked around. All clear.

"Right?" asked Josh.

"Right!" said Olly. Maybe things would soon turn out all right.

They set out again, this time retracing their steps but still alert to signs of people or sounds of horses. The countryside seemed deserted, villagers and farm workers staying in their cottages or hiding in case they were forced to join whichever army saw them first.

25

Josh glanced at Olly who shrugged and shook his head. Neither really knew what to do nor what they'd find when they returned to Bankhouse Hall but those thoughts accompanied their steps.

As if matching their mood, a dark cloud appeared and moved steadily across the sky. More billowed in the distance and the wind blew harder. Thunder rumbled overhead.

"Can you go faster?"

Olly nodded and picked up speed. Neither wanted to return to the deserted home but neither wanted to be out in the open when the storm broke.

The wind gusted around them, pulling at their clothes, teasing their hair and chilling their hands. As the cold began to bite their hunger became fiercer. They knew where to find shelter but they had no food? Nowhere felt safe.

A crack and a flash startled them both. The roar of thunder followed almost immediately. They knew the storm was almost upon them but they daren't stop and shelter. Another flash and a crack and they saw the top of a tall tree break and fall. The sound of branches crashing through the lower boughs mingled with the drumming of the thunder. They still had a long way to go.

"If we get really wet we'll leave footsteps through the house..."

"... and a trail of drips." Josh finished his sentence for him.

"Well," Olly stopped to think. "Well, we could hide in an outhouse... or a shed."

"I think they'd check they were safe. It's the first place they'd look."

Olly nodded. Josh was right, as usual.

They plodded on. The wind rose and the first drops of rain fell. The boys hurried but knew they had no chance of beating the storm.

As the rain fell more heavily and, as their clothes got wetter and heavier, their going got harder and the boys took less and less notice of their surroundings.

"Hey! You! Stop, you two."

They gaped at each other. They had forgotten to be careful. The sound came from behind them. They turned together. A man stood on a lane near three tiny cottages. Was he a soldier or a villager?

"You two. Come here." He called again and beckoned.

Josh and Olly looked at each other and decided together. They faced the way they had to go and ran.

The man yelled again but they couldn't hear him. When Josh risked a glance back he was still standing where they'd first seen him.

They reached a small copse and charged into it, ignoring the brambles grabbing at their clothes. They stopped in the middle, panting. Olly bent over clutching his side, breathing hard. Josh clasped a hand to his ribs where they hurt from the effort. He looked all around. No one had followed them. They were safe for the moment but he knew they could not stop as cold soon seeped into their damp clothes. Josh knew they had to move on.

"Olly, are you all right?"

His friend nodded.

"I've got to go. It's not so far now. If we can get inside, we'll be out of the rain."

Olly nodded and straightened up. "We've got to find shelter. I'm okay now."

"You ready?" Josh waited for a nod and led the way.

They continued the few paces through the trees. It was still raining though not as heavily. The storm had passed so the wind had dropped too but now mud caked their boots. The ground was sodden and slowed their progress. They struggled to cover the distance to the hillock that had hidden them before.

Again they approached carefully, anxious to see if their way was clear but also scared they might attract more unwanted attention. They saw no one so crept over the rise ready to race back if anyone appeared.

26

The house was as quiet as it had been when they'd last entered. As before, they checked the sheds and outhouses. While Olly needed convincing that no one else was there Josh wondered if there were any safe hiding places. They entered through the kitchens and though they searched again, there was still no food to be found.

Olly followed Josh through the ground floor. "We'd be safer upstairs. If someone ... when someone comes, we can see who it is... or decide if we need to hide."

"Good thinking." Josh led the way to the stairs.

"Can we see the hall from the doorway to the attics?"

Josh looked around. "No, but if we stay by this room, we can reach the steps without being seen. We'll open the door so we can make a quick escape."

They settled to wait and, out of the wind, their clothes began to dry and as they did, the boys felt warmer. That wasn't good for it made them feel sleepy.

Josh stood up abruptly and nudged Olly with his foot. "Get up. We've got to keep moving. We'll get caught if we go to sleep."

Olly was about to answer when they heard the noise of bridles tinkling and hooves stamping. Someone had entered the hall when they weren't listening. The horse sounds were coming from outside and they heard someone inside shouting commands to people on the doorstep.

"That doesn't sound like Captain Harry... and it's no one I recognise." Josh whispered.

"If they're Sir Roger's men... they'll trap Captain Harry unless we can warn him..."

Olly grabbed his sleeve and they crept to the attic steps, sliding along the wall. At the foot of the steps they waited. Josh held the door ready to close it if someone climbed the stairs.

More voices rose from the ground floor and bodies in the hall doorway blocked out the light. One voice rose giving orders.

"We need to move." Josh pulled the attic door shut and they tiptoed upwards, hurrying until they came to the room with the secret panel.

Olly tugged at his friend's arm and pointed. "We need to scuff out these footprints."

Josh nodded. Their tracks led straight to the panel. He pulled off his jacket and dragged it over the floor, spreading the marks so that it looked as if several people had pulled at the chest and searched the room. When he was satisfied he nodded to Olly who was waiting by the opened panel.

"Shh!" Olly gestured and Josh stopped abruptly, listening. Footsteps, several sets, marched from the stone steps along the attic corridor.

"Quick," Olly beckoned through the opening and moved over for Josh.

Josh reached the opening and slipped as he tried to clamber through. In his hurry, he had cracked his head on a crossbeam. He lay half in, half out of the secret hole.

Olly grabbed him under the arms. It was difficult to pull him into the narrow space but he heaved and twisted until he finally pulled Josh in.

He reached over to pull the panel shut and, as it clicked into place, he heard the attic door pushed open so hard it crashed against the wall. They couldn't hear words at first, only the tramp of feet on the wooden boards and then silence. How long could they hide there? How long would he and Josh be safe?

The muffled voices continued but the boys couldn't make out words until one voice boomed out silencing the others.

"This is my house now. Those boys were seen heading in this direction. Where are they? I want that boy. Joseph

Banks will lead me to his captain."

"That's Sir Roger Bolchester. We've got to get out of here. We must warn my troop." Josh's head ached from the bump but he was resolved. He knew they needed a new plan.

27

The boys stayed in their hidden place until all the noise of the Cavalier soldiers had died down. Then they opened the panel a tiny crack, letting in some light but also any distant sounds. After an age, they swung it fully open then waited again.

"We're not taking risks. Not any!" Josh had feared Sir Roger, now he hated him. "If Sir Roger gets me, my company will be forced to try and save me... and Captain Harry may be killed."

They couldn't stay where they were so Josh crawled out into the attic, stood slowly and listened. Olly followed but said nothing. He knew Josh was right. He knew they had to warn Josh's company or they'd never be safe.

"If we can get out... and we can find Captain Harry... he'll know what to do... I think. He was supposed to come here."

The boys stared at each other. Josh nodded towards the doorway and they crept across the floor testing each board before putting any weight on it. There was still no sound.

"Do you think it's safe to go further?" Olly tried to control his voice.

Josh was just as frightened but made up his mind. "If we can get out of the house we stand a chance of finding help. Even if Roundheads capture us, we must persuade them we have information for their leader..." It was half a plan.

"Yes, but we've got to get past those soldiers first. It's quiet now... but does that mean everyone's gone?"

"I'll... we'll have to find out. We can't climb out of this attic. We've got to go down the stairs. I'll lead."

Josh crept into the corridor and stopped every few paces to listen. He inched his way along keeping close to the edge where the boards wouldn't squeak. He halted at the top of the stairs to listen again.

After a moment he looked back to Olly and whispered to him, "Stay there. I'll go to the foot of the stairs and stop at the door. If everything's quiet, I'll open it a crack."

"What if there's someone?"

"Then we have to get back into that secret hole."

Olly nodded and watched as Josh inched his way down to the servants' door. He held his breath as Josh squeezed the handle and turned it slowly, carefully, until he could see a sliver of light.

Josh waited for a long moment then opened the door a

crack big enough to get his eye to. There was no one for him to see so he beckoned Olly to follow.

Olly had descended four steps when he slipped. His foot skidded off the front of the stone. He threw himself backwards and managed to sit on a step instead of pitching forwards.

Josh's mouth opened and it stayed that way until Olly whispered, "I'm okay. I won't do it again."

He watched anxiously as Olly edged down and joined him by the door. He let out his breath. "We must get to the next stairs."

He waited for Olly's nod and they set off, once more keeping to the sides of the corridor. Half way along, they heard a gust of laughter but it came from behind a closed door so they hurried on. The back stairs were stone so there was no risk of noisy footsteps as long as they were careful.

They barely breathed until they'd left the house behind and cleared the distance to the gate in the wall. They were still free.

Josh pointed out the hillock with shrubs on. "Over there."

The boys ran, dived through the bushes and fell flat, panting. They were free. They'd left the Cavaliers behind in Bankhouse Hall but they had a difficult decision to make.

28

Josh was still worried. "We know Sir Roger's not there. Those soldiers are hungry... I don't think they'll guard the house properly..."

"Yes, but they know your captain's due there... We've got to be careful."

"Sir Roger must have a spy... He's really wicked. Where do you think the captain is?"

"They stared at each other then Olly said, "What can we do?"

"We stay here till nightfall. We're hidden for now... then back the way we came."

Neither slept. They waited through the dusk then, with moonlight, they moved to the edge of the scrub.

"We'll make for that copse we hid in then see if anyone else is moving."

Olly only mumbled.

"Let's go." Josh tugged his friend's sleeve and Olly followed.

They reached the patch of woodland and crossed it then stopped at the far edge. It was beginning to get light when they looked for other movement.

As soon as they felt safe Josh again said, "We'll hide in that haystack again" and they raced across the open land.

Huffing and puffing they scrabbled at the loose straw and dived into their hiding place. They were panting so hard they didn't hear the faint footsteps. A hand pulled their cover away and reached for them. Neither could speak.

"Shh. I'll not hurt you. Show me your faces." The hand grabbed Josh's ankle and pulled at him.

He smacked it away. "I'm coming." He swallowed hard.

"And you." The man waited for Olly. "You needn't cry. I'll not harm you."

"He's not crying. It's straw dust." Josh tried to be stronger but the hand now clasped his arm and he couldn't get free.

"Quiet. Be still, the pair of you. I need to see you properly. I'll not hurt you." He pulled them both into the full daylight then grinned.

"I thought I recognised you running towards Bankhouse Hall. I tried to warn you."

"You shouted at us?"

He nodded to Josh. "You've met me. My name's Luke. I'm one of Captain Harry's advance guard. I sent a runner to say you'd been spotted."

"Why?" Olly spoke.

"We won the last battle. One of our prisoners was overheard talking about two boys. You were the only ones we knew of. Everyone's been anxious about you."

"We've been trying to find our families," said Olly.

"Or Captain Harry Smithson," added Josh.

"The company is on its way... should be here quite soon."

"But there's Cavaliers in the Hall." Josh had to save them from capture.

"They're hiding upstairs," said Olly.

"Oh, are they! Good work, you two."

The boys hadn't noticed another soldier join them. Luke turned to him and Josh recognised Matthew, the lieutenant he'd last seen when he'd been captured.

"Get back to the troop. Tell the Captain the boys are safe and that Bolchester's men have prepared an ambush in Bankhouse Hall. You heard the details?" Luke instructed.

"Yes, sir." Matthew nodded at Josh and disappeared as smoothly as he'd come.

29

The boys waited for several hours until the sun was high in the sky when they finally saw troops approaching the haystack. Josh recognised Captain Harry, with other officers beside him. Luke and Matthew were riding near the head of the column.

Josh threw himself at Captain Harry as soon as he'd dismounted.

"Captain Harry..."

"It's all right, son. We got your message. I will mount an attack from the side. Matthew will lead an approach from the drive as if we think we're safe."

Josh and Olly both protested.

"It's all right." Luke interrupted. "Matthew will attack first. That will confuse them. Captain Smithson will overpower them just when they think we're outnumbered. They won't expect it."

Captain Smithson nodded then added, "You boys stay here with Luke until it's safe."

Luke protested. The boys argued. Their protests were useless. They were ordered to remain. As they waited, all three wondered what was happening inside the house.

At last word came, and, with Luke now following, they arrived at Bankhouse Hall.

Captain Harry met them outside. He nodded to Olly, turned to Josh and said, "You've done well, lad. My company will take those Cavaliers to prison. Pity Sir Roger Bolchester escaped but he's lost most of his men and his castle. He'll hang when we catch him. The Parliamentarians have won."

"So I... we're safe from Sir Roger?" Josh waited for his captain's nod. "I always wanted to be a Roundhead. I knew I had to help them win." He grinned at Olly and sighed with relief.

Captain Harry patted him on the shoulder. "Well done, lad. You've earned your place. Let's go in. Show me where you hid." He saluted the boys then signalled the column of prisoners to move off.

Josh raced into the hall with Olly close behind.

They were greeted with, "Are you hungry? Tell us how you found out Sir Roger's plans... but eat first."

Some time later Josh groaned. "I didn't know I was that hungry."

"Or me,"said Olly.

"We'll show you where we hid." Josh pulled the Captain's arm and the boys led the way to the attic.

"There's a secret hiding place. It's behind that big box."

Olly raced Josh to the trunk and together they pulled it away from the panelling then opened the secret door.

"We'll show you. Come on Olly."

They climbed into the secret chamber and shut the panel.

"Hey." Olly tugged at Josh's sleeve. "It goes further. I think there's a tunnel."

But before they moved they heard a distant noise and voices calling.

"We'd better get back," said Josh and they squirmed their way back to the tunnel entrance.

*****

Olly found the place where the tunnel ended and fumbled for the catch to open the panel. He wished he had a torch. He really needed one now but was not sure how he'd thought that. He panicked when the panel refused to open. His palms sweated as he ran his hands backwards and forwards over the wood.

Josh reached across him. "How does the catch work? Let me try..."

"Don't worry. I can do it."

"How do you know?"

"It's too hard to explain. Back up a bit."

Josh flattened himself and Olly shuffled closer to the

opening side. He felt for the space where the door latch sat in the frame, stopped to take a slow, careful breath, and opened the secret door. Both of them inhaled the fresh air of the castle and looked around. The attic had disappeared.

They saw a panelled room and grinned at each other as they recognised their surroundings. They clambered out, grimy from their scramble, and gasped at the welcome that greeted them.

Josh's parents stood there with a police officer, a large dog and a woman. Olly recognised the castle manager.

They heard the officer speak into his radio. "You can step down now. The boys have just appeared. I'll check they're okay then report in."

"Dad. Mum."

"It's good to see you, lad." His father clasped Josh in a tight hug before his mother pushed him aside and pulled Josh into her arms.

"And Oliver!" He was hugged too.

"How clever... you found the priest's hole. Seventeenth century... Everyone knew there'd been one but the secret of the entrance was lost years ago..."

Josh's parents ignored the castle manager.

Mr Banks nodded to the police officer. "Questions later?" After a nod he made a decision. "We'll phone your parents, Olly. Let them know you're safe, thank goodness..."

"We've been so frightened," Mrs Banks interrupted.

His father continued, "...so all that Civil War research paid off. We'll go for a pizza then you can explain... tell us all about what happened."

The boys grinned at each other. They'd a lot to think about. Josh gave Olly a nudge and winked.